Samara the Wholehearted

NANCY BAUER

Samara the Wholehearted

GOOSE LANE

Published with the assistance of the Canada Council and the New Brunswick Department of Tourism, Recreation and Heritage, 1991.

Cover art: "Return to the Day Haunt of the Siffleur Montagne" by Peter Bell, 1986, acrylic on masonite, 122 cm x 110 cm, Permanent Collection, Art Gallery, Memorial University of Newfoundland.
Back cover photo by Monte Draper, Bemidji *Pioneer*.
Book design by Julie Scriver.
Printed in Canada by The Tribune Press.

Canadian Cataloguing in Publication Data

Bauer, Nancy, 1934-
    Samara the wholehearted

    ISBN 0-86492-103-9

    I. Title.

PS8553.A837S35 1991   C813.'54   C91-097665-1
PR9199.3.B3757S35 1991

Goose Lane Editions
361 Queen Street
Fredericton, New Brunswick
Canada E3B 1B1

*For all the aunts of this world
and especially for five perfect examples:
Gladys Bridgeford Angus, Tempie Luke Blanchette,
Kimberly Keddy Bauer, Reba Lockerby Luke
and Elsa Bauer Wimmer*

Summerland

1

The unaccustomed light wakened Samara early. She pulled on her sweatsuit, not bothering with underwear, took her sneakers in her hand and quietly opened the sliding glass door. Stevie and Sophie had stayed overnight, a sleep-over to celebrate the first day of the summer vacation. Samara could hear their regular breathing and knew they were still asleep. This was the first time she had not wanted to come to Summerland, but the red sun on the horizon, the great blue herons feeding in the backwater of the river, the still seas that only last night had been pounding surf, pleased her in spite of herself. This would be her last summer here, she'd told her mother and father. At the river mouth, a fishing boat was putting out to sea.

Stevie and Sophie had caught her mood, and the three girls had taken turns last night complaining about these isolating summers, away from friends. But they were luckier than she was. They would have visitors over the summer. Fredericton was only two hours away, and there was even a bus from the city to Newcastle. But there was no way her friends could visit — twelve hours away by car or a bus trip of nearly two days.

She'd struck a bargain with her parents. They would pay

for a plane ticket for Roger from Boston to Moncton, and he had arranged with the other guard to swap — do two shifts so each could have a week off.

Samara had come out on the deck thinking she'd write a letter to Roger, but instead she put on her sneakers and went down to the beach. She sauntered along their shore as far as it went and then waded into the water so that she wouldn't have to climb the bank and be in sight of the Richards' cottage. Past the point of land dividing Summerland from the Richards' property, a little cove made a naturally-sheltered beach about forty feet long and thirty feet wide. The cove was a magical place for Samara: here she saw no land before or behind — she saw only the Northumberland Strait stretched out in front of her. Samara sat down with her back against the sand bank and watched the ocean. Here she was beyond the scrutiny of her mother and father.

Once, several years ago while on a Christmas visit to Fredericton, her parents had decided to make a trip to Summerland. They had come along an almost deserted road, had a near-accident, and when they arrived, found the place desolate, cold, and gray. To get to the cove Samara had gone across the Richards' property and down their wooden stairs. The little beach was littered with driftwood, a styrofoam buoy, a wooden box, and the carcass of a dead animal. Had the ocean taken them all back or had the Richards cleaned it up themselves the next spring? Or maybe they, like the Bellmonts, hired someone to get the place ready for them.

Having made up her mind that this was her last year at Summerland, she could begin the process of "this is the last time I'll . . . " One of the things she would miss was the excitement of meeting the people who rented the two spare cabins and the bedrooms of the farmhouse. This year the excitement was even greater, because her surprise half-brother and his wife and two children were coming for three weeks. Samara had only learned about this man a few months ago when he'd written to say that his mother had confessed to him that his biological father was Conway Bellmont. Now he was coming from Ohio to meet this real father.

Samara was excited, but she was uneasy as well. It wasn't that she was afraid this man would replace her in her father's heart. And Conway had made sure that she knew the brother's age so she would see that the birth had occurred during his bachelor years. But the brother could be bringing with him some other revelation, of what kind she couldn't imagine.

Her body was chilled when she got back to the cabin, especially her wet feet, so she took her pad of paper and climbed back into her sleeping bag, still retaining its warmth, her warmth.

> *Dear Roger,*
>   *Only one day away from you and already my heart is sick with missing you.*

She drifted off to sleep and awoke with Sophie's voice, "Are you two going to sleep all day? Breakfast will be over in half an hour."

The three of them dressed quickly in the blue sweatsuits that had been unofficially adopted as Summerland uniforms many years ago.

"I'll see you up there," Samara said as Sophie and Stevie peeled off at their cabins.

She walked across a field and through a small copse of hemlock trees to the farmhouse. This year the cook was new, the daughter-in-law of their long-time cook, Teresa. The new woman, Rose, was married to Gerard, Samara's first crush, at age thirteen when he was sixteen. Samara could still blush with shame over the way she'd thrown herself at him that long-ago summer.

Her mother and father were finishing their breakfast, lingering over coffee, waiting, Samara was sure, to see if she came for her breakfast. She thought for an instant of not sitting with them, but then she decided that the pleasure of the gesture would not be worth the explanation that would be requested.

"How was your sleepover?" her mother said.

"All right."

"Just all right?" Carol asked.

"It must be natural to outgrow your friends."

"Not natural to outgrow them in one year, I wouldn't think," Carol said.

"Maybe outgrow is not the precise word," Conway interjected. "But certainly people mature. Sophie and Stevie lead lives quite different from Samara's. And her interests have changed the last few months."

"Not for the better, in my humble opinion," Carol said.

"If we're going to argue, I'll move over there. You know how I hate arguing at breakfast. My stomach gets all churned up."

"Why be provocative then, when I just asked you a polite question, along the lines of how do you like the weather."

"The weather's not too great either. Damp and cold. No wonder you've got arthritis."

Conway stepped in again. "We've had confirmation that Fred is coming. With his partner — I don't know whether she's his wife — and his two children."

"I suppose you'll be embarrassed. Or aren't you going to tell people who he is?" Samara said.

"Why be embarrassed. Of course I'm going to acknowledge him. I have no reason to suspect his mother of lying."

"Money," Samara said.

"That's being more cynical than I care to be. And of course you know that what he's told me on the phone is quite convincing."

"Aunt" Penny, head down and forward, arms swinging, in a concentrating walk so characteristic you could spot her from far away, was just now appearing out of the path through the hemlock copse. She and Sophie usually ate their breakfast alone together in their cabin, while Penny went over the logistics of the day. "Uncle" Philip would come the twenty-first of June for his two months' holidays, returning to Fredericton as business called.

"Aunt" Nita, Stevie's mother, had come and gone from breakfast. "Uncle" Paul had not yet arrived at Summerland, He would come erratically and leave just as unexpectedly. There would be others, too, coming for varying lengths of time. But Samara's father, Conway, was called the Sultan, because he was sometimes the only male among his harem.

Rose had gone all out for this first breakfast — popovers, sausages, eggs baked in cream. Samara felt cheer and homecomingness creeping up in her, ready to outflank her gloom.

After her father purchased the farm, he'd had the house remodeled, mainly by knocking out walls. What had been a living room and dining room, two rooms on the front of the house facing the ocean, became one big dining area with a long table that ran the width of the house. There were two fireplaces, and often on a cold rainy morning there would be fires lit in both. On the back of the house, facing the road, was the large kitchen, pantry, and summer kitchen and across the hall a small sitting room for the help. The four bedrooms upstairs were for people coming to the Institute. These people tended to gather around one end of the dining table to socialize.

When they gathered for a class or for exercises, they met in the barn, a building they all considered special if not sacred. It was round and made of fieldstone. But since Samara had grown up in it she didn't have quite the spooky feeling about it that her parents had.

They kept reminding her of how much she had loved Summerland when she was small by telling her anecdotes in order, she supposed, to fill her with nostalgia. One of the stories she had heard so often, she could almost scream when she felt it coming on, about the time she was five and they were packing up to go back to Boston. She had stuffed a plastic breadbag with her hairbrush, her bathing suit, and her guinea pig, who had miraculously escaped suffocation, and set out to find Teresa to ask if she could stay with her for the winter.

At Summerland she could wander at will and spend much of her time with other children. There were always special events, unusual food, youngsters from the town who were urged to visit so that the Summerland children could practice their French. Storms roiled the sea, even on two occasions a hurricane. There was always the surprise of new people. The Bellmont living room was naturally a centre for more intimate conversations, philosophical, administrative, or merely gossipy. Samara knew from very young, as all only children do, how to camouflage her presence.

She was rather old to be rebelling, even if her complaints were mild. But she'd been so closely bound to her parents that it seemed inevitable she would need a sharp break. Rebellion had been built into their schemes for her upbringing, but they'd been sure it would occur around twelve or thirteen, possibly sixteen or seventeen, so that when she had reached the age of twenty, they had decided she just was not the rebellious type. Her mutiny this spring, her determination not to go to Summerland, although sad, in one way reassured Carol. She'd been watching for spunk, so that when spunk manifested itself, Carol could not be unhappy.

Although it was only the first full day they'd been

there, the adults had opted to begin their daily schedule. Samara had declared that although she was to spend the summer there, she would not participate in the "absurd activities." Instead she luxuriated in the pleasure of not having anything she had to do, of having a whole unregulated summer for the first time in her life.

But in spite of herself, she was curious about her newfound half-brother. He might help her to understand her father. Already, the idea that Conway had once had an affair resulting in an illegitimate child made him seem more real, more human. Her mother had once described him as a seraph, which she said was a fiery kind of angel, not the sweet kind pictured at Christmas, but a somewhat terrifying creature doing God's bidding whether comforting or ferocious, yet still not of this world.

Her mother, on the other hand, was altogether too real, too human, too overwhelming a personality. She was overprotective, she knew everything, she was always right. The fact that she was knowledgeable and right made her a heavy adversary. And because Carol was wise, she must be aware she was overwhelming, Samara knew. She knew too that her mother had truly been disappointed when the university had not received funding for the summer project and Samara's job had fallen through. But somehow that didn't make having to come back to Summerland any more palatable.

Would this brother look like her? She did not look like either her father or mother. They both were tall, imposing people. She was prettier than her mother had been at her age, but her mother was then and was still now stately, standing with her elbows out, her feet apart, her face lit up with her exuberance for life, as if her eyes were perpetually open wide, her mouth always in a startled gat-toothed grin. Samara didn't look like her father either. His head was large with most of it above his eyes, with high flat cheek bones, and a perfect nose. Her train of thought came to a familiar but unpleasant stop. She was inferior to both her parents in every way, except that she was pretty, and not even an interesting pretty at that.

She had to decide what she was going to do. She could, she thought, go into the kitchen and try to resume her French, and certainly if it had been Teresa there, she would have. Or she could walk along the beach and up to the village to renew old acquaintances, but that would be more fun to do later with Sophie and Stevie.

What a boring summer this is going to be, she thought.

Her mother and father had gone into the barn last night and had invited her to come along, but she had declined. Now, she began to feel a certain desire to see it. What was it they were doing in there now? Centering? The dancing exercises? The music? That music was so familiar to her that she was always surprised — and pleased — when guests expressed their feelings of the unfamiliar, the eerie. Sophie would have chosen the coveted thumb gourd. Or maybe the cactus whistle her mother had found in Cambridge. Stevie loved the music and played with gusto; she might be playing the new whistle.

Now, sitting on the farmhouse steps, Samara could imagine what they were doing in there. She could picture them as they all did the tai chi a visitor had taught them ten or twelve years ago. She could picture the earnest, concentrated look on Stevie's face as she awkwardly but determinedly did the moves. She would be standing next to her mother, Nita, who, thin and birdlike, was doing the exercises as if she'd been born to do them — effortlessly, gracefully. Aunt Penny would be smiling, enjoying the sight of them all, their individuality, as she did the tai chi movements matter of factly. She seemed not to have become an iota better at them in all those years. Sophie would look at her mother and grin, but after a few minutes her own concentration would be greater than Stevie's although with less effort — at a certain point a veil

14

would drop over her face, her movements would become more fluid, almost as if she were sleepwalking, or underwater.

Samara's mother, Carol, took everything with a grain of salt. If tai chi helped one or two to concentrate, fine, but she didn't expect it to help her, Samara knew. Her mother was large, arthritic, and the exercises sometimes caused her pain. But, she also thought that this kind of exercise, like swimming, helped her joints. She would look relaxed.

Her father, Conway, was remarkably athletic for seventy-eight. People were always amazed at his age, and whenever anyone tried to guess that age, the person would be off twenty or twenty-five years. Sometimes Samara thought him brilliant, a genius, with supernatural powers. But sometimes she heard him tell something she knew to be untrue, or saw him bluff, and then she worried that her good opinion was totally false. He was still a mystery to her.

Uncle Paul was mysterious too. Samara had confided in Stevie her doubts about Conway, and Stevie, amazed yet relieved, had in turn confided her doubts about her own father. Where did Paul go when he went away two or three months at a time? Why wouldn't he tell them if it was on a legitimate quest? Did he have another woman? Was he a criminal, a spy? When Stevie asked her mother, she just said, "It's for a good cause, I'm sure. Don't bother him about it."

After the tai chi chuan, they would centre, Samara knew. Then they might focus on a number or a letter or they might tell stories, always Samara's favourite activity. They never did the same routine twice — there were ten or twelve activities and they would do four perhaps, always including centring.

Samara got up from the steps and strolled over to the barn door. When she heard them stir, knew that centring was over, she would go in. It would be a shame to miss story-telling. After the long separation, they would all have good stories to tell.

2

On Friday afternoon a van rolled into the farmhouse driveway. The driver, a large young man in his late twenties perhaps, got out.

He opened up the side door to operate a hydraulic lift. In the wheelchair was a woman of indeterminate age, probably in her thirties, physically drawn in upon herself so that she seemed tiny. Her thin face had a hooked nose, buck teeth, and a beatific shy smile. Her eyes, though sunken into her skull, nevertheless were bright with life and intelligence. The young man was gentle with her and entirely competent in manipulating the wheelchair. Samara, lingering over her lunch in the dining hall, waited for someone else to come out of the barn to greet the couple. But no one appeared, and the two, looking around to see what to do next, were so appealing that Samara relinquished her vow not to have anything official to do with Summerland and went out to greet them.

"I'm Samara Bellmont. Can I help you?"

"Ron Trembath. This is Marty Peters. She's here for the summer."

The woman made a sound. The man translated, "She says she is very excited and happy to be here."

"We're happy to have you. Did you have a good trip? Have you come far?"

"Yes, a long ways. St. Paul, in Minnesota. But we've had a good trip. We took our time."

The woman made another sound. "She says this is the first time she's ever seen the ocean. We've been catching glimpses of the water for quite a few miles. At first we thought we'd get out and have a good look. But we decided it would be better to wait until we got to Summerland."

"You must be tired and hungry. I'll go get the others. They're in the barn. We didn't know Marty would have a wheelchair, so we haven't put up the ramp yet. It's always taken down in the winter to preserve it better. But they shouldn't take very long to get it up. And in the meantime, we can all have supper in the barn. We love an excuse for a picnic. Come this way."

Samara, hearing the silence, opened the door gingerly and then shut it quietly.

"They're centring now. It won't take long. I'm not sure how they've arranged things for you. Aunt Penny is usually in charge of accommodations."

"That's certainly an unusual barn."

"I think that's what attracted them to the property in the first place. Even before the ocean. What drew you here?"

"Her really. I'm just along for the ride. Although everything she gets interested in, naturally I do too. Except that most of it I don't understand. She's what you might call a genius." The woman murmured. "She says I'm making her embarrassed. But you are. They'll learn soon enough. All the same, it saves a lot of hemming and hawing. She's a research associate at the University of Minnesota. She heads up a research project. I went to work there as a lab assistant after I got my degree. And for some reason, I was on her wavelength right off the bat. So they made me her assistant. It's great for me because I'm right at the heart of all the research."

The woman made a sound again. "She says I haven't answered your question, that I'm rambling. I do that. But I'm learning not to — she's teaching me that. So what is your interest? You tell her."

More sounds. "She says when Mr. Bellmont came to speak at the university, we went to hear him. His talk was on how to deliberately create synapses in the brain. Afterwards there was a stimulating question and answer period. She thought this would be a perfect vacation — by the ocean and a stimulating atmosphere, but still away from St. Paul and the lab."

Sounds of movement came from the barn, so Samara opened the door, and said, "Dad, Aunt Penny."

Outside, her father looked perplexed. "Dr. Peters. What a wonderful surprise."

"It shouldn't be a surprise," Ron said. "We did register."

Penny said, "M. Peters? And R. Trembath? Yes, we have you registered. I didn't realize you knew Conway so I maybe didn't mention your names. I'll call the carpenter right now — it will only take a little while to put up the ramp. And the farmhouse has an elevator to your rooms."

While she was inside calling, Ron walked up and down, surveying the scene. "I suppose it wouldn't be possible to have one of those cabins down by the ocean."

Conway spoke. "Certainly. Cabin one would be the best one, I think. I'll have a walkway constructed over the rough part in the lower field. It's something we've been going to do for a long time. It won't take more than a few hours. And in the meantime I think you can manage. If it rains and makes the path unnavigable, we'll hold the meeting in your living room and have your meals transported down there." Penny reappeared. Conway explained his plan to her. "What do you think?"

"Perfect. We'll talk to the carpenter when he gets here. Come get the key, Samara, so you and your father can show them the cabin. I'll be down in a few minutes to check things out."

The first evening Samara offered to bring to Marty's cabin the hot chocolate and cookies that traditionally ended the evening activities at Summerland. She knocked at the sliding glass door and saw Ron come out of the bedroom.

"This is terrific. I was just saying to Marty that I wished I had a bedtime snack. It must be ESP. Come in. I'm just getting Marty into her nightdress. We'll be ready in a minute."

When he summoned Samara, she came into the room with the tray. The room had been rearranged so that the foot of the bed was flush against the sliding glass door.

Marty was sitting up in bed, leaning against a donut-shaped pillow that seemed tailor-made to keep her in one position. An extension arm was clamped to the headboard, and from it branched several devices. Marty, pressing a button, manipulated one of the devices, a cup-holder, to enable her to take sips of the hot, now warm, chocolate. She was wearing a pink flannel nightgown with a ruffle around the neck. She looked comfortable and relaxed; Samara realized only then that all day Marty had been more nervous and physically uncomfortable than she was accustomed to being.

"I'll give you this," Ron said to Samara and held out a small metal box. "It's an alarm. We've never needed it, but it will make me feel better if you have it. Marty thinks it's foolishness. She feels we're being too much trouble. But having her here will be worth any amount of trouble."

Marty murmured. "I'm embarrassing her. But she's only kidding, aren't you? You know your own worth." Ron reached out and stroked her hair, smiling fondly at her. "God's gift, and no mistake."

As they talked, Samara began to understand Marty's sounds. She had thought, during the day, that she'd understood several words, but now, in the peace and quiet, with Marty looking so happy, and Ron obviously relieved to be over the hurdle of getting things arranged, Samara realized that some of the sounds were becoming more intelligible; whether Marty's relaxation made them more so, or whether Samara herself was getting adept at interpreting them, she didn't know. At one point as Ron was about to translate, Samara said, "I think I know. You said, This is a beautiful place."

Ron looked pleased. Marty smiled, her lips pulling crookedly away from her buck teeth.

"Marty says it's like learning another language," Ron said. "Some people have the facility, others don't. But you sure are speedy."

"I'll go now. I'm sure you're both tired. I'm bringing

your breakfast down tomorrow. What time will you be getting up?"

"Marty's determined to watch the sun rise over the ocean. So anytime after daybreak!"

In the twilight, Samara walked back along the shore, carrying the tray. Nita's and Penny's cabins were lit up, the curtains not closed, so that Samara could see first Nita and Stevie at the card table playing, she guessed, *Lord of the Rings*, and then Penny and Sophie reading. At her own cabin, her mother and father were talking. They had a fire in the woodstove, and they were both in their pyjamas. Samara said, stepping into the room, "I think I'll be able to understand her quite soon."

"That's very good."

"What is it she does exactly?" Samara asked.

"She's a mathematician working in particle physics. Up until the arrival of this young man, Ron, she'd been dependent on her aging mother. And totally confined to St. Paul — between her house and the university. So I think maybe this is a trial run to see if she can travel. And she was obviously intrigued when I told her about this place — the beauty of it, our activities."

"He has to undress her."

"I expect so."

Before she went to sleep, Samara moved her bed flush with the glass door so that she too would wake to the rising sun. She put a chest under the mattress to raise it up. She found it impossible to sleep on her back that way so she had to take the chest out.

At seven in the morning the sound of hammers began, but when Samara came with breakfast, Ron was still asleep. She let herself in with her key. Marty smiled to see her and said, "Ron is a ___ sleepyhead." Samara didn't get the word.

She said, "I should wake him up. Unless I can help with your meal."

"If you don't mind helping. He ___ ___ break."

Samara plunged in, arranging the coffee cup in the extension arm holder, and positioning Marty's arm in the sling. Marty used a tweezers to pluck her food. Samara felt her heart warming, swelling out towards the woman for her courage, her cheerfulness. But when Marty started to cough, Samara became nervous, and she went to wake up Ron. "Ron, it's time to get up," she said gently.

He leaped out of bed, his eyes still shut. He was wearing nothing. "What is it?" he said. And then "My God. My dream is still *there*. I was flying like a bird, but a string was attached to me and the further I flew, the tighter the string got. Oh yes. There it is — what I was flying over. The ocean. A storm over the ocean. What a queer thing. To be awake, up, and still dreaming."

"Marty is coughing," Samara said.

"That's all right. I'd better get some clothes on before I get arrested."

While Ron took a shower and got dressed, Marty continued to eat her breakfast, assuring Samara that there was no danger, that the coughing had been routine.

On the way down the path from the farmhouse, Samara had wondered if she should deliver the food and then leave, or if she should stay and have breakfast with them. She did not want to intrude. Nor did she want to be unfriendly. At Summerland, some people had breakfast alone in their cabins, others took it in the dining hall. By the time Ron was ready for his breakfast, Marty had finished hers. Samara had another decision to make. Should she leave or stay while Ron had his breakfast. Ron solved the dilemma.

"Shall I tell Samara some of your story?"

Marty murmured. "She says I exaggerate." Marty made another sound. "She says you can understand her?"

Samara nodded. "Some of it."

"That's surprising, isn't it? People who have known her all their lives don't understand. And it took me several weeks." Marty made a sound. "Several months. Marty's father" and Ron took a sip of his coffee, "was a physicist too. And when he discovered that she had inherited this disease — his mother had it — he wanted her to have something she could concentrate her mind on — something that wouldn't need anything outside. So he began to teach her the math of particle physics. She was six when he began. He wanted her to have plenty of corn to grind, he said — I like that image. He didn't want her mind to be grinding away with nothing to work on. She says that when she was young, there would be whole afternoons go by when she would have nothing in her head except a mathematical function."

At 9:50 the Chinese gong was sounded to call people to the ten o'clock morning exercises. Samara, sitting in the wicker swing that hung from the ceiling of her room, reading *Emanation*, felt a strong temptation to forget her declaration that she would not participate in Summerland activities. Not least of the tempting reasons was her curiosity as to how her father would modify the program to include Marty. Marty might be disappointed at the silliness of the activities. She might regret the expenditure of energy and time it took to get here.

She shut the book and hurried outside and up the path, overtaking Stevie and Sophie. Stevie said, "I win!" And Sophie, grinning, said, "She bet you'd come this morning. That Ron's so handsome."

"I am coming. But it's not on account of him. I just find Marty interesting. He's not so handsome anyway — his nose is too big."

"Maybe his nose is big, but haven't you noticed his body? Yeow!"

Samara was not going to say anything about the morning's incident, and she hoped he wouldn't either. Already she felt a distance about his nakedness as if he had been an ancient statue.

During the centring, the usual quiet of the farm was broken by the hammering on the walkway being put in

place. The thud of the hammer was followed by its ringing
and then by the echo, five regular thuds and then a pause.
When Samara was little the former owner was still alive,
still living in the farmhouse, and he kept a cow in the
barn. In the evening the centring would occasionally be
punctuated by the cow's lowing. Then, too, there was
sometimes the smell of new-mown hay in the barn.

At home, very rarely, their centring would be disturbed
by the doorbell ringing. Samara would look at her mother
and father; they seemed not to notice the sound at all, and
when centring was over and Samara said, Shall I see if
someone is still at the door, they would seem surprised.
She asked her mother, Didn't you hear the bell? Her
mother said, I suppose I did, but it was so far away that it
didn't seem to have anything to do with me. Another time,
Samara had asked, What if something was wrong? If I was
dying or the house was on fire? Would you hear? This
departure from life frightened her; she herself would
always be more alert, on guard. But her mother had
assured her that if Samara had screamed, she would have
heard.

The excitement of having these interesting new people
and the ringing of the hammer would not trouble her
mother's and father's concentration.

For the physical activity her father had chosen isometric
exercises. Conway put on the tape recorder, and rhythmic
deep growling sounds were overlaid with a groaning
melody played by a bassoon. Conway's soothing voice
murmured out the directions: left little finger. Throat,
kneecap.

Samara couldn't decide if was because of Ron and Marty
that Conway announced a storytime or if it was for her,
because he knew what she liked. Once, when she was
much younger, they had storytime every morning and
some evenings. But it was so difficult for the regulars to
come up with a different story. And some of the guests
would tell interminable pointless anecdotes. So the group

decided to have storytime only twice a week. Samara liked
this activity not only because she enjoyed listening but also
because she enjoyed telling, and knew she did it well.

Nita began. She told a story about Stephen, the
legendary blind photographer, tragically killed in an
accident. Nita often told stories about him, always when
Paul, her husband, was not present. She even invented
incidents to keep alive his memory.

Samara volunteered to go next: "An exchange student
from Ruwanda told me this story. In his village, for
centuries, no one knows how long exactly, one man is the
spiritual leader. Usually the position is handed down from
father or mother to son or daughter — no distinction is
made of the sex of the leader. But sometimes the leader has
no children or the children are not worthy, and then the
village must determine which person will be the leader. Of
course in a small village everyone is related to everyone
else, everyone has the genes of a spiritual leader in him.
During the times when the succession is irregular, there is
great excitement and great danger. People, even though
fearful, are stimulated, and very often progress is made,
new songs are discovered, new ways of doing things. The
spirits — the ancestors of the villagers — help them to
determine the leader. The spirits put signs on the chosen
one. Soon all the people know who should be the leader.
No one is proclaimed who doesn't have the full support of
every single villager.

"Some of these signs are interesting. There's always been
a school in the village. In the last hundred years the school
teacher has taught not only their own language but also
English and math. The spiritual leader as well as all the
adults sit in on the class at least three or four times a year.
They're looking for a sign. But the sign is not that the
student is the smartest or the best. That student might
become the next teacher, or the representative to the
government, or the head of the food co-op. But the sign
they are looking for to indicate a spiritual leader is a sense

of humour. The youngster who makes everyone see the funny side of things has a mark on him. The younger the person is, the more sure the mark."

"Are there other signs?" Penny said.

"Hundreds, I guess. To be a leader you don't have to have all the signs. But you have to have the sense of humour. They call it the 'breathgiving.' The student I talked to was the son of the representative to the Ruwandan government. He said he was allowed to come to America because he had none of the signs. Or not many. Some of the other signs I remember are if you had a reddish tinge to your hair, or were left-handed, or had an extra finger or toe. If a lizard would walk up your arm, if insects didn't bite you. Or if someone's headache went away if you put your hand on his head.

"The great leaders, the legendary ones, could move houses. If the community decided a building should be moved, all the adults would hold a night-long vigil and at dawn the spiritual leader would go into a trance. If he is a great leader, the house moves. My friend had never seen a house move, but his father had. The spiritual leader gets in touch with the ancestral spirits, and they move the building."

"We usually have three stories. Does anyone else want to tell one?" Conway asked.

"I'll tell one," Ron said.

Marty's head went up, and Samara, observing, was sure she was apprehensive. It was, Samara thought, typically American to offer a story the first day. Canadians would wait a day or two; New Brunswickers would wait two weeks.

Samara could not tell whether Ron's choice of story pleased or bothered Marty, and it was only many weeks later that Marty confessed she'd been embarrassed.

"Once upon a time," Ron began, "in a far-off land, St. Paul, Minnesota, there lived a boy, Ron Trembath."

Samara observed the corners of her mother's mouth turn

up, and she knew why. It would often happen that a
newcomer would start his story thus, and the regulars
knew he thought he was being original and clever. Usually
the storyteller carried on the device for a few sentences.

"This boy felt from a young age that he had a destiny to
fulfill, that he'd been born for a purpose. When he was
older, twenty-six, a series of coincidences showed him this
destiny. He was assigned to the lab of Marty Peters. The
first thing he discovered was that they shared the same
birthday, April sixteenth, and the same middle name, Chase.

"Then one Friday in late November the two people who
took turns coming to get Marty got their signals crossed.
Marty got quite worried when she realized that the
building was emptying, leaving her there. She waited
patiently, not wanting to use her emergency button or
telephone her mother, who had a heart condition. As long
as she got home by nine, she knew her mother wouldn't
worry — would think she'd had a meeting or was visiting a
friend.

"I had gone home from my afternoon lab, but when I
got there I kept having a feeling that I'd left something
undone or forgotten something. I went over in my mind,
remembering, and was sure I'd turned off lights, unplugged
things. But by then the feeling was so strong, I couldn't
resist it, no matter how hard I used my reason. I'll have no
peace, I thought, until I go check. So I went, saw Marty's
light on, went in to see what she was up to. I had not
spoken to her much and still didn't understand her, but I
did realize she was worried and needed someone to take
her home.

"That was the first event. Of course I thought about the
feeling I'd had to go back to the lab. It had been a queer
incident. But it was after the second event that I knew I
was being led to my life's work and this time I actually
heard a voice. In February, the driver of her van slipped as
he was opening the door and tore a ligament in his ankle.
He was in agony and nearly fainted. It was at the back of

26

the Institute building, near the freight loading. Marty was out on the ramp, it was cold and the wind was howling. Her emergency button was inside her jacket. She's very susceptible to cold and wind — it literally takes her breath away. The driver hollered for help, but no one heard.

"I had left ten minutes before and was walking to the bus stop across campus, a good half mile away. And I heard someone calling help. I thought it was Marty's voice. At first I thought — you're hearing things, Ron old boy. But I heard the voice again. So I turned around and ran back. I could see the light in our lab wasn't on, so I ran around the back and there they were, in such a pickle. Marty said afterward that she'd been calling for help, but not out loud. I knew then, in my heart of hearts, that taking care of Marty was to be my work. But I resisted it. Because naturally I had thought my destiny would be to make some great scientific discovery. Or if not that, do some daring deed. But the next August her mother died. There was a lot of talk around — who was going to stay with Marty. There were several people who wanted to — some of her disciples. And of course there were some who thought I was unsuitable — a man. But I saw this big jigsaw puzzle with one piece missing and I was just that shape. So I popped myself in."

He had not, Samara noticed, said anything about love.

Samara assigned herself to be Marty's and Ron's assistant. On rainy days she brought breakfast to their cabin. She helped Ron translate Marty's words.

Four days after their arrival, Ron came down with a virus. He had a stomach ache and diarrhea. He was terrified that Marty would get it, and even though everyone assured him that she had already been exposed to the virus, he insisted on moving out for a day. Samara exchanged rooms with him. Marty made her promise that they would call in a nurse if Marty got the flu. Ron would insist on caring for her, Marty said. But she knew there was a limit and diarrhea was it.

Samara had thought about the details of Marty's personal hygiene. How did she wipe herself after she'd gone to the bathroom? Did she have a period? Did Ron attend to all that?

Samara's mother, Carol, was a wonderfully thoughtful nurse when Samara was sick, and she could imagine Ron's being treated like a king. That pleased her. Carol had said to Samara, "You know, I wouldn't worry about Marty getting this flu. Ron's been caring for her without a break for many weeks. It's possible that this is his body's way of getting a little rest. I wouldn't say this to anyone else. I don't think we have to borrow trouble."

Samara usually slept deep and immediately, but the unaccustomed responsibility kept her restless. And then there was the disturbing presence of Ron — his clothes slung carelessly around, his odour (was it aftershave or what?), his little row of books on the built-in dresser, touchingly naive, Samara thought, for his stay at Summerland: *The Tao of Physics*, Swedenborg's *Heaven and Hell*, and *What Science Owes to Mysticism*, plus three detective stories.

The night, however, passed without incident, and Samara was still dozing when Stevie came with their breakfast. Samara found herself being glad it was Stevie and not Sophie. She was accustomed to analyzing her feelings, especially surprising or irrational ones: Was Stevie less of a threat to her own importance?

No, that was not it. More subtle than that. It was that Stevie was likely to have a deep empathy, her own life having been so up and down. Stevie would not be nervous about dealing with the care of Marty. Maybe she would have had to care for her own mother in one of Nita's "spells."

Marty told Samara that she would love to have a bath, but she didn't want to be a bother, that she'd already been such trouble. But Samara understood that the mere mention of Marty's desire was a compliment to herself. Marty, she realized, accepted as sincere her offer to help. And maybe Marty even understood how her arrival had turned Summerland from a nuisance to a challenge. Carol might even have mentioned it. Yes, that was probably it.

After their breakfast, Stevie drew the bath while Samara undressed Marty. Samara realized then that Marty had not been out of her nightgown for over thirty-six hours. Samara wheeled her into the bathroom, took off the sheet she'd put over the naked body, and with Stevie's help, lifted Marty off the chair onto the toilet. Ron had arranged a tray-like apparatus between the toilet and the sink on which Marty's arm could rest, supporting herself, and protecting her from falling.

The two girls left her and went into the bedroom and sat on the bed. Stevie reached out and took Samara's hand, squeezed it, patted it with her other hand. Samara returned the squeeze. It had meant, we'll handle this somehow, and she appreciated the gesture because she was troubled. How much should she offer to do? Offer to wipe Marty's private parts? She didn't think she'd mind. She was quite sure that all the training in centring, concentration, self-discipline would keep her from flinching, gagging, whatever. But would she insult Marty in offering? Ron should have been more explicit in his directions.

They heard Marty speak. "She's ready," Samara said.

When they lifted Marty off the toilet, having flushed it, Samara saw toilet paper disappearing down the drain. Stevie put her elbow into the bath again, to double check, and then they gently lowered Marty into the water and onto the inflated plastic chair. Stevie said, "Call me when you need me," and went into the bedroom. How thoughtful and sensitive she is, Samara mused. How lucky I am to have been surrounded with the cream of the crop all my life.

She took the soft facecloth spread out on the side of the

tub and soaped it generously. "Like this?" she said, and lifting Marty's leg, straightening it gently, began to soap it, behind the knee, between the toes. She proceeded this way, concentrating totally — behind the ears, the back of the neck. She lifted first one breast and soaped under it, then the other. There was silence, except for the water's sloshing. Outside sea birds were probably cawing, but in the little bathroom, no noise penetrated. Samara could see Stevie sitting motionless, silently on the bed. Marty's laboured breathing began to soften, quiet, become more regular.

Samara's hands no longer felt as if they were hers. Touching Marty's back, her hands seemed to melt into Marty's skin. She worked slowly, rhythmically, soaping the facecloth, washing the left arm, methodically, soothingly, then rinsing the facecloth and rinsing the arm, once, twice. Kneeling there in that awkward position, she felt no discomfort, and touching Marty's pubic hair, not a shred of embarrassment.

Samara leaned out over the tub, and stretched her right hand, grasping the soap-holder handle. With her left hand she slid Marty slightly up and over her arm, and reaching down, lifting Marty's buttocks up, Samara washed carefully, sloshed rinsing water over the skin. There were scabs there, she could feel, and probably rashes too. "Lord have mercy," she prayed for the first time in two years. "Lord have mercy. Heal these sores."

The next morning Carol came to visit just as Stevie was leaving with the remains of breakfast.

"Before you go, Stevie, let's discuss this. Ron says he's all better and can come back. In fact he's very eager. But I was thinking, maybe one day of recuperating would be beneficial. What do you think? Can you all manage without him?"

Marty murmured. Samara said, "Marty is all for his having another day as long as I don't mind. She's afraid he's getting run down because he never has a day off."

"I don't believe he thinks of taking care of you as a job, so he doesn't think in terms of a day off. But practically speaking, as Marty has told us, it is a responsibility, and no matter how much you love your work, you do need a break," Carol said.

"I'm having a great time and learning so much. I'd love to stay another day," Samara said.

"And you, Stevie?"

Stevie looked surprised. "Oh I'm not doing anything. And it's so nice having Samara back to her old self."

Sweet Stevie. So like her mother, Samara thought. Always blurting out the unvarnished truth.

Samara was, in fact, Marty said, her first girl friend. The twelve years between them made no difference. She had not always been this disabled — hers was a progressively worsening disease — but she'd always been isolated, and as a child ostracized. Samara should know what precious gifts her beauty and her strong supple body were.

"I don't think there ever was a more one-sided person than I am," Marty said. "Whenever I'm awake in the night or alone or even in a ___ my mind is working on a problem. But I need something to push me onto another track. Your father's visit to the university and Ron's taking over of me were a fortunate coincidence."

Late that afternoon Conway came to help maneuver Marty to the dining room and then to the barn for the evening activities. Carol and Ron were missing. But there were two new people who must have arrived that day. One was a thin man, nearly emaciated, with a sparse beard. "He looks like Jesus Christ," Samara whispered to Marty. His companion was a squat, substantial woman in sensible shoes. They were, it turned out, brother and sister, recent immigrants from England, they explained. They said little, but that little was in a heavy Russian accent. After Marty was introduced to the pair, she said to Samara, "From an icon."

Penny was in charge this evening. Samara noticed that

Sophie also wasn't there. Perhaps she was bored with whatever activity her mother was proposing. It was not a new activity, as it turned out, but an old favourite, theatre games. In "Where are we going?" it was Marty's idea that she and Samara be going to Hell, and she provided convincing sound effects of fire crackling.

But this precipitated hiccups which everyone could see were distressing for her. "Home?" she said to Samara. And that was the first word the others had understood. "I can manage, Dad," Samara said. "It's all downhill."

Back at the cabin, Marty sipped sugar water, and the hiccups stopped. "I'm hoarse," she said. "From talking so much. And very tired. I'll go to bed now." She wanted the drapes closed too, so that the light wouldn't wake her. Samara, closing them, saw Sophie and Ron walking down to the beach. Before she went out of the room, she stopped to stroke Marty's hair and say goodnight. "I'm very comfortable and happy," Marty said.

Samara plugged in the hotpot to make herself some green tea. She got into her nightdress and propped herself up with the pillow so she could sit looking out to sea. It was still quite light, but even when it began to get dark, she did not put on the lamp. She was physically tired, but her mind was whirling. What an amazing thing it was that this woman, because she could do nothing else, had spent all her time thinking math, and thus had arrived at a place few people ever had been before. This was the concentration her mother was always going on about. But Carol had not achieved one half of what Marty had achieved. Samara began to imagine herself being that one-track-minded about something and thus winning The Prize. The sadness of Marty's life, the thorough isolation — Samara her first girl friend — had played such an important part in Marty's achievement. Even if Samara wanted to, she could not lead such an eremitic life.

She dozed, and when she woke up, the moon was just

lifting itself out of the sea. Samara drew the drapes on the astonished moon and slept deeply.

3

Uncle Philip was coming this afternoon, and except for occasional short trips back to Fredericton, he would stay for the rest of the summer. He always brought with him an array of technological wonders which everyone at Summerland got to use. Philip had worked for a computerized information centre and eventually bought the Fredericton franchise. Sophie recently told Samara that Conway had helped Philip buy the business and was a silent partner. Samara had not said anything to anyone else because Sophie was telling her a secret.

The carful of technology Philip brought with him allowed him to run the business from a distance, in just a few hours a day. Last summer the piece of equipment that most intrigued everyone was a portable computer the size of a paperback book. This computer was plugged into a worldwide network of magazine publishers. The contents of each magazine were elaborately cross-indexed so that if Samara wished to have information on any subject, she typed the word and received a list of current articles. She then selected which ones she wanted, entered her billing code, and over the screen would come the article, simultaneously translated if the article was in another language. The company was in the process of computerizing the articles of back issues. Samara and Sophie had spent $700 reading articles on everything from methods of increasing the efficiency of the brain's synapses to the genealogy of the Bellmonts.

They were anticipating the arrival of Samara's half-brother on Wednesday, but he arrived on Tuesday, having made better time than he'd expected. He did not look like Conway, yet he and Samara both had a family resemblance to their great-grandfather, Conway suggested. Fred, however, was plain, even unattractive, while Samara was beautiful. The difference was partially in their expression: Fred's was blank at best; he was too fat, not the growing-old fat of a once athletic man with a beer belly, but the pudgy all-over fat of a sissy. And even though he was thirty-nine, he still had a bad case of acne. His partner had a take-charge air of complete competence.

Because Summerland was run rather like a school or a summer institute none of them had the mechanisms handy to greet pure visitors. The routine had to go on as usual because of the other guests, and meals still had to be communal. Yet these routines and activities provided common grounds for talk and speculation. Fred's wife pitched into the discussion and exercises with enthusiasm. Fred sat silently by, looking embarrassed and uncomfortable. Conway, usually at ease, found himself in the strange situation of not knowing what to say, how to behave. Towards his son, a man should show affection, but Fred kept that at bay.

Fred had decided to seek out his father because he thought Conway might be able to shed some light on his problem: he could see into the future. He had tried to hide this ability, to ignore it. He was frightened and confused by it. If Conway had any doubts that this was his son, they disappeared. For it was the preternatural — not supernatural — ability to see into the future that had made his grandfather wealthy. No one in the family since then had had the gift — or curse.

It was difficult to get time and place to have intimate conversations. On Friday evening, they were to have a barn dance, inviting the townspeople, and Conway suggested to Fred that they eschew the dance to have coffee in his cabin and talk. When Samara heard about this appointment, she asked Fred whether he minded if she attended too.

"It's like this, Mr. Bellmont."

"Call me Conway."

"Yes, of course. Mr. Bellmont is rather formal for a father."

"And yet father is too much of a shock."

"A big shock. This is the way it works. As I am looking at something happening at the moment, the picture kind of slides, or maybe elongates is a better word, into the future. This sliding thing occurs without warning. And not often — once every three or four months. Something like that. And the other thing is that the picture slides and stops, but I don't know how much time has elapsed. I mean I don't know when the final picture I'm seeing actually will take place — one week or a hundred years."

"You can't control it," Conway said.

"No, in no way."

"What kind of picture? I mean is there a certain kind of picture that the sliding happens to?" Samara asked.

"Yes. It's not like science fiction, you know. Not like picturing something that doesn't exist now. And not like seeing an event — I've read about that. Someone coming to an intersection and getting a picture of a horrible accident which happens there in a day or a few months. Not like that. It's more as if I were looking at that stove and the picture kind of fast forwarded like a videotape until I could see what it would look like in the future."

"But how do you know your picture isn't just imagining?" Samara said.

"I think it is imagining — a funny kind of imagining."

"And the place won't necessarily even look like that?"

"Oh no. It will look like that. I mean I've checked up. I've described the changes on paper, and then months or years later I can confirm it. A friend of ours had a son and when he was fourteen he was quite homely and misshapen

— very short, fat, with a peculiar shape — arms too long, a posture that was almost like a humpback, face rather plain. His mother was quite troubled because he was so unhappy. And sitting at the table after dinner — the boy had just left for hockey practice — I had the sliding experience — and saw him quite good-looking — the bones in his face or maybe the muscles — had hardened, got bolder, and he looked quite manly. And he'd grown — not a real tall man but maybe five feet eight — and become muscular. He radiated confidence, vitality. And seven years later, there he was, as I had seen him seven years previously."

Conway said, "My grandfather used to practice, exercise this gift, I think. He determined what circumstances would most likely induce this seeing, and he would put himself into that situation and try to start the thing rolling."

"Was your grandfather nervous? Afraid of it? It sounds like he wasn't."

"No, I don't think he was afraid of it. Are you?"

"Yes. Until I was twenty-six, I had convinced myself that it was just idle daydreaming. But then an event happened — not dramatic but unmistakable. I was standing in the window looking across the street at the convenience store, and the sliding — the elongating — happened. It stopped at the store having become something else — exactly what I couldn't tell but much more elegant looking. And sure enough, six month later the store was sold and became a beauty salon."

"So you could have made a modest profit by buying it then and selling it six months later."

"I suppose so. Although it never would have occurred to me to do that. Another thing that happens is that the picture sometimes slides back the other way — goes forward and then back. And on a very few occasions goes forward again."

"And you see the same thing?"

"No, different. The same but different — a different

angle. But when that happens, I can't remember much afterwards. I feel very confused."

Conway said, "Does this sound familiar, Samara? Anything like this going on in your head?"

"No, not like that. But I do sometimes feel I know what people are thinking."

"That could just be normal empathy, couldn't it?

"I suppose so."

"Do you have an explanation for all this?" Conway asked.

"No. I don't. I was hoping you would," Fred said.

"Of course I've thought about it a lot. I never discussed this with my grandfather — everything I know came second-hand, mostly from my father. One of the problems I think is that we don't have a word that describes the phenomenon. All the words we'd usually use have the meaning of "before" — you are now at this moment seeing something before it happens. Pro, pre, fore — all those prefixes that mean before — foretell, premonition, prophesy. And your description suggests to me that you're witnessing it as it happens. You are going beyond in order to see it. Our words tend to keep space and time quite separate. And now we know of course that time is just one dimension of space."

"You're right that the words aren't adequate to describe what happens. I've used slide and elongate, but they are not satisfactory words."

"Grow? Expand? Develop?"

"No, none of those exactly. Smoother than those. I'll try to think of a word, although heaven knows I've tried many times before."

Fred was an enigma for his father. Conway told Samara later that he couldn't decide whether his innocence and humility masked his intelligence or if he indeed was a little slow. Conway's grandfather had been a strident, cocky man, and physical presence, charisma, had marked his father and two uncles. To have such a strong family resemblance in a person of an entirely different stripe was eerie.

Five days after Fred arrived, his car was gone, and he appeared at lunch with his two children and without his wife. By supper she'd not returned, nor by the end of the next day.

"Is your wife going to be away long?" Penny asked.

"Oh, she's gone for the remainder of our time here. She's driven to Halifax. She'll pick us up on her way back."

It was, Penny said to Samara, as if Fred's wife had stayed long enough to check Summerland out as a responsible babysitter for Fred and the children, and then took the opportunity to have a vacation. "If she is his wife," Samara said.

The children, Gina, eight, and Gus, six, were well-behaved, quiet, and they often appeared holding their father's hands. But, Carol said to Samara and Conway, it was as if they were holding his hands so that he wouldn't dash out in front of a car.

Now dinner was boisterous and gay, with fifteen people around the table: Philip, Penny and Sophie; Nita and Stevie; the Russian brother and sister, Yuri and Raisa; Fred and his two children, Gina and Gus; Marty and Ron; and Conway, Carol and Samara. Rose was not as good a cook as Teresa was, but she was more adventurous — variety and surprise compensated for a less than sure hand. A tough, dry pot roast would be accompanied by samphire greens. Or medallions of veal in supreme sauce would be followed by a failed chocolate cake.

Conway marveled at the concatenation of events that had brought seven such innocents into conjunction. He felt cleansed, he said, by the atmosphere of tranquillity and purity in those first few weeks of Summerland.

Samara, Ron, and Marty were a constant trio. Samara

was so absorbed that it appeared she was avoiding Fred.
Carol intervened.

"Your dad feels bad that you avoid Fred. He thinks you
blame him for having this half-brother."

Carol had taken a calculated risk. Samara might go on
the rampage again. But she didn't; she was surprised that
her behavior might be interpreted in this way, and she
offered to make an effort to talk to Fred.

She was up and dressed the next morning, ready for a
walk, when she saw Fred picking his way down the rocks
toward the grotto. Samara's first reaction was to go the
opposite way, towards the river, but remembering her
mother's words, she set off in Fred's direction. When she
caught up with him, he was standing in front of the grotto.
It had been built into the overhang of a steep bank. The
builder had used a natural indentation, but he had
excavated it and had built a structure of fieldstones and
beach rocks large enough for two or three people to enter
at once, although they would have to stoop to get in. At
the far end, a slab of slate made an altar.

"This is an amazing piece of work," he said, smiling at
her.

"Isn't it! Did my father tell you about it?"
Simultaneously she regretted her words "my father."

"No, no one has mentioned it."

"We used to come here more often before we made the
beach. The shore was all like this — rocky. But we picked
up the rocks and hauled in sand over there to make a
beach. So now the poor grotto gets lonely."

"Did your father make this?"

"No, the man we bought this property from — his
father made it. He wanted to do something to match *his*
father's barn. He got the idea from the grotto out on the
main road. But he made this one better. The one out on
the road is hardly a grotto at all. When I was little, I used
to sneak in here and pretend I was a knight in a cave."

"Does this all belong to your father?"

Samara said, "You could say 'our' father, because he's your father too."

"That's difficult to get used to." He smiled.

"I bet. I can't imagine how I'd feel. What a shock."

"Does Conway own all this?"

"I don't know. I don't know what you'd call it. He seems to be the one to get things done. But I think it's kind of jointly owned. I'm not sure. I think they kind of all bought it together way back. You've met most of them. But you haven't met Paul. I hope you get to meet him. No one ever knows where he's been or what he's been up to. And how does he make his living? Sophie and I think maybe he has another wife and family. He could be a spy. And handsome. My God. He must be fifty years old but he's all muscles. He sometimes wears a long robe down to the ground, made of otter fur. And another robe woven of white with beautiful embroidery and a hood."

"Where does he wear these robes to? Is he a minister or what?"

"Here! He wears them here. And God knows where else."

"You've certainly lived a different sort of a life, haven't you?"

"I suppose. But most of it is pretty ordinary. Have you lived an exciting life?"

"No, not really. Kind of a sad life I suppose. I was pretty much ignored as a kid. Spent all my time with nannies and day care. I understand why now. My mother and father travelled a lot, led a high life. And now, well to tell you the truth, all I long for is the ordinary. My wife and my children. Not to be lonely. Already I feel better, talking to your father. Our father. He makes it seem less scary."

"Do you want to go inside here? We try to keep it up, but it gets pretty battered in the winter."

They hunched over and entered the grotto. She opened the waterproof container, took out a wooden match and lit the fifteen votive candles sitting on the slate altar.

Samara, preoccupied with Marty and Ron, had not yet walked up to the village. Sophie and Stevie had gone twice and reported it unchanged except for a new Yassa canteen. Gerard's younger brother had grown and matured and was now the ultimate, although shy. That evening Ron did not like the supper, and after the activities he proposed to drive to the village to get a hamburger.

"Want to walk instead?" Samara suggested.

Marty urged him to walk, saying she'd be fine. To relieve his mind he could leave the alarm button with someone — Carol volunteered. Marty said she could use a few minutes to herself.

At the Seagull Restaurant, Samara recounted the story of her grand passion for Gerard, the number of times she had walked to the village, the way she hurled herself at him. "I still feel as if everyone must be laughing at me when I walk into the restaurant."

"I've had flings but nothing serious. It always was such a pain in the neck — meeting the parents, where to go Friday night, how to find the money, what to buy for a birthday present."

"But isn't it exciting? I mean there's such a shivery feeling when there's someone new. Life is full of possibilities."

"Maybe there's something wrong with me. Something left out. I'm not gay — if I had to chose, I'd chose a girl. And sure, there's pleasure. But it's outweighed by the pain. Girls are so difficult to understand."

On the way home, it had gotten dark so that they had to walk close together, crowded onto the shoulder of the road.

"Be careful. It's kind of tricky around here. There's a brook." Samara took Ron's hand and led him slowly along until they'd passed the culvert. Then she didn't know whether to drop his hand, which now was also clasping hers. She relaxed her grip a little, but he did not take the hint.

"Here's the path to the Richards'. Do you want to take

the shortcut? I can show you a special place of mine. You have to get your feet wet — I think the tide is in."

"Sure. Why not?"

They picked their way across the field and down to the cove.

"You can't see anything but the ocean. The Richards are here only on the weekends usually and even when they're here, they can't see anyone sitting up against the bank."

They sat down. "This *is* a special place," Ron said. "Look at the stars. It's like we're alone in the universe."

Ron put his arm around her shoulder and hugged her to him. "We're like Adam and Eve," he said.

"And Eve was so much trouble."

Ron laughed. For fifteen minutes they sat huddled together in silence, listening to the rumble of the sea, before they got up to leave.

One hundred and fifty feet away on the other side of the point, Fred squatted on the rocky beach and shone his pipe lighter into the grotto. Carol had found a reliable teenager to babysit so that he could attend the evening activities and "have some time to yourself." On the way back from the barn, he'd looked in the window and seen them happily playing a game, so he'd gone for a walk along the shore.

The votive candles were still there on the slate altar so he lit several. The red glow of the candles gradually became green. The green glow took shape, gathered form to itself. It was a bird, a parrot-like bird with a large hooked beak. The bird wore a mantle of woven cloth, black with an intricate cross embroidered in gold thread. The bird spoke, a raucous squawking.

"Shh," Fred said out loud. "Everyone will hear you." But the squawking seemed only a clearing of the bird's throat, as if he hadn't spoken for a long time and was not sure what would come out if he uttered sounds. The voice lowered, became sweet and enticing. "Let not your heart be troubled, neither let it be afraid. Your heart, your heart, your blessed heart," the bird said.

Fred was crouching there while the green glow faded, became reddish again. There were voices, comforting voices, happy voices, splashing sounds. His knees were stiff. The splashing sounds ceased, but the happy voices came closer.

"Fred, hi," said a surprised Samara.

He turned his head. "Oh. It's just you. Are you walking back?"

"Yes, Ron and I have been to town."

"I heard that. I'll walk with you."

He blew out the candles and waddled out of the grotto. As he stood, his knees crackled. "I'm stiff," he explained. "I'm getting old. Or maybe it's just the dampness."

He felt lightheaded. But he also was infused with peaceful, contented warmth. Spontaneously, he took Samara's hand and kissed it. Then he took Ron's hand, and swinging arms and grinning, the three of them walked home.

4

Yuri and Raisa were causing a scandal. The cleaning lady, pausing outside Raisa's bedroom, heard unmistakable sounds of love-making. She and Rose discussed the matter and decided Carol must be told.

"We saw no one else going up or downstairs except her brother."

You couldn't really confront adults with such information. Perhaps they, like Abram and Sarai, were not really brother and sister, but man and wife, or lovers. Or had their enforced isolation driven them to this?

They participated in the morning and evening activities, but unenthusiastically. They rarely spoke, during the events or after. They whispered together during meals, in Russian it seemed. They went on long walks together.

Then, several days after the cleaning lady's revelation, Samara came back from her sunrise walk and knocked on her parents' bedroom door.

"You guys decent?"

"Yes, come in."

Conway was sitting up in bed reading; Carol was stooped over the coffee machine, pouring coffee.

"Want a cup?"

"Sure, why not," Samara said. She sat on the bed and drew her legs up. "Dad, you look so comfy."

"I am comfy. I'm looking out to sea, I'm warm, I smell the coffee, and I have a wonderful book to read. It's as close to Eden as humans ever get, I think."

"You guys sure know how to live the good life. Contentment is the main ingredient."

They fixed their coffee with sugar and cream, and Carol passed around nut rolls.

Samara said, "I saw a strange thing this morning. A very strange thing. I was walking up the river bank to see the herons, and out of the woods came Raisa and Yuri. They didn't see me, but they were heading in the same direction I was. I was going to shout and catch up with them, but then I realized they were holding hands."

"Yes?"

"Well, isn't it kind of odd for a brother and sister to hold hands?"

"Maybe it was rocky or something, just there. He was helping her," Carol said.

"No, it wasn't that kind of holding hands."

"Actually — don't say a word of this to anyone else — but your father and I were just beginning to suspect that they aren't brother and sister."

"Why would they pretend? What would be the point?"

"That's what we wonder about too. But perhaps it's something to do with Immigration."

"Yeah. That could be it. Relatives can get in but not lovers. That makes sense. But they weren't being very discreet."

"They didn't expect you to be out so early, I imagine."

"They're kind of spooky anyway, don't you think? Ron was saying they act like spies."

"I do think we should make a greater effort to draw them into the group. They seem like such outsiders, so lonely," Conway said.

"True. But they act as if they really don't want our company."

"That might just be shyness. Or not knowing our customs."

"Maybe I'll go up to breakfast now. I know they eat awfully early — they're always finishing when I get there."

Yuri and Raisa were standing at the buffet table spearing sausages and pancakes when Samara came in.

"Hi! I guess we're the early birds that get the worms."

The two looked perplexed but both nodded.

When Samara had chosen her breakfast, she sat opposite them. "So, how do you like Summerland? The place, I mean. The physical spot."

"It is very beautiful. Very peaceful," Yuri said.

"Isn't it? My father says it's as close to paradise as humans ever get. Me, I'm up and down about it. I've been coming here so long there aren't many surprises. And the activities in the barn seem so routine now."

"We do not find them routine. On the contrary, we find them difficult to understand," Raisa said.

"Difficult to understand what is going on at the moment and difficult to understand why. The purpose. The purpose for these games eludes us," Yuri said.

"Isn't that funny. And to me they seem too obvious. Too calculated."

"Perhaps you can tell us then," Yuri said, "what is the

meaning of the game in which we hop about on one foot, and then we have a partner and hop about and then try to make our two single legs act like a pair and walk. It seems to be a game for children."

"But it's fun, don't you think? The reason for it though, is — I'll ask my mother and father to make sure I've got it right — is that two people can act as one. That two one-legged persons can walk like one two-legged person."

"I see." Yuri paused. "But what is the wider purpose of this? Why would they want us to walk as one?"

"They say that all these things are experiments — seeing if you can make a family-type group out of people who are not related. A substitute family for people without one."

"Perhaps they have invented the analogy that brothers and sisters get to know each other through playing, through shared experiences," Yuri said. He was a small, thin man who looked to be seventeen or eighteen, but who certainly must have been older. He had a sparse beard and the ecru smooth skin of one who had been seriously ill. He seemed more at home in the English language than his sister, although she spoke with less accent. Raisa had a broad, square head and slightly dumpy body, but the vitality showing through her face and figure was translated into physical attractiveness.

"Did you expect something else when you came here?" Samara asked.

They looked at each other, perplexed, whether over the meaning of her question or over the answer, she couldn't tell.

"We are here for recuperation. A friend of ours, Edward Barnhart, perhaps you remember him, recommended it."

"Eddie! Yes, of course I remember him. What a character. What's he doing now?"

The remainder of their breakfast time was spent exchanging stories of this Edward. Later, Samara said to her mother, "Did you know it was Eddie Barnhart who sent Yuri and Raisa to us? I had a long talk with them at breakfast. You know, I don't think they're brother and sister at all."

"Why do you say that?"

"Just a gut feeling, I guess."

Thursday was sleep-in day with no morning activities and brunch served from ten until one. Early birds got a thermos of coffee and some rolls after Wednesday's evening event. Sophie and Stevie invited Samara to a sleepover for Wednesday night. "We hardly get to see you at all," Sophie said, and Samara detected hurt in her voice.

When Sophie was eight or nine, her grandmother had given her for Christmas a board game, *Cross Canada*, the object being to get from one end of Canada to another, using various modes of transportation and having adventures on the way. The three girls had begun to keep score, and then a journal, of the times they'd played, now nearly six hundred games. One summer they'd each adopted a persona as a traveler, and, making up new cards, they'd added that further complication to the game. They had a record of each trip, going back seven years when they'd decided to keep the journal. Keeping the record at first had been an outgrowth of their parents' zeal for journals, but later, more irreverent, they had turned the journal into a parody. The last two years, they had used it for their philosophical speculations.

Now they were about to play the first game of the summer, and Sophie made tentative comments that showed she wondered what attitude to adopt. Back to the good old days of hilarity? Of course now they were too old to take the philosophy seriously. But Samara set the tone.

"You know how I felt the first day? Well, here I am doing a complete about face. We've been lucky, you know, to have been brought up here. So much love, so many wonderful people around. Marty has made me see that.

Even this game — just think of how much of our thoughts
and fears have been poured into it. We were educating
ourselves and didn't even realize it."

Their evening was one of remembering. At every move
they consulted the journal back over the years. Their
parents would have been amused to see their deep yearning
at only twenty for the lost past, a nostalgia for the Golden
Age.

"Remember last year when Stevie started the game with
a non-stop flight from Charlottetown to Toronto?" Sophie
said.

"And I spent fifteen days rowing a dory from Port au
Basque to Sydney," Samara said.

"But that wasn't the fastest game," Sophie said. "Here's
one four years ago that only took twenty minutes."

"Was that the one where Samara sold me the winning
lottery ticket?"

"Yes. Can you remember how much the ticket was
worth?"

"One million dollars!" Samara said.

"No," Stevie said. "Sophie won a million. I only won
half a million. But it was enough."

Of course they knew when the next card was going to
be one of their homemade cards (written on cut-up juice
boxes). And now, in the first game of the season, the first
appearance of one of their own cards precipitated a song in
the air.

The next morning, that song was still present. Samara,
waking with the first light, heard not words, only vibrations,
but she understood the meaning: childhood was over, and
if she did not hasten to write down her recollections, they
too would go. Even now, the everyday magic was fading
from her memory, and only individual strong events
remained vivid. Yet, had she tried to get it down on paper
last year, she could not have done so, because then she was
still a part of it, still not self-conscious enough.

But that had been one of the aims of her upbringing and

of Summerland: to submerge the ego, to achieve a true community, a true Kingdom of Heaven.

She had so immediately become attached to Ron and Marty, felt that she comprehended them. And she was proud of how quickly she'd solved the mystery of Yuri and Raisa. She was even beginning to develop an empathy with Fred.

"What good do we do?" she'd asked her mother, arguing to be allowed to stay in Boston.

"For one thing we keep alive the possibility of such a community. Of course we'll never reach perfection, but someone has to keep the idea alive, and not just the imaginary idea, but the practical working out of it — how such a community can be created."

Yuri and Raisa always wore long-sleeved shirts and jeans. Even after the hot weather set in, they continued. Samara speculated with her parents, "Maybe it never gets warm where they come from, so they don't own any summer clothes."

"They could roll up the sleeves," Carol said.

"Some people don't mind the heat," Conway said.

But on the fifth of July, the temperature rose fiercely; there didn't even seem to be a sea breeze. Marty suffered and could do nothing but lie on her bed in a cotton nightdress and hope that a breeze would come through the open door. Philip and Ron went to Moncton to buy an air-conditioning unit and some other supplies for Marty. Samara sat in a chair next to Marty's bed, reading out loud a biography of Trevor Lowe. From her place she could look down the shore to where Raisa and Yuri were paddling in the sea, their pant legs rolled to the ankle. After a while, they found a shady place against the bank and sat resting there.

Suddenly, Raisa jumped to her feet. "Oh, oh, oh," she whimpered.

Samara went to the door. "I'll just go see what's the matter with Raisa," she said to Marty.

Raisa had sat against a wasp nest in the bank and now wasps were stinging her, on her feet, on her scalp; they even seemed to have got inside her blouse. Yuri stood transfixed in horror, wringing his hands. Samara leaped over the bank and began brushing the wasps away. Raisa was shaking her head, so Samara parted the hair and plucked out wasps, crushing them between her fingers as she flung them away.

Raisa kept slapping her shoulder and chest.

"Take off your blouse," Samara commanded.

"No, no."

"There's no one to see, no one at all." Samara reinforced her opinion by looking up and down the beach.

Raisa looked beseechingly at Yuri. "Yuri. Yuri," she moaned.

"He'll turn around," Samara said.

"No, it's not that," Yuri said. "It's you. She does not wish you to see."

"I'll turn around. You get the wasps then."

"He must not. He must not! He's allergic to them. Don't touch them."

"You get them out yourself. Take off your blouse and brush them away." Samara turned to face Marty's cabin. She heard Raisa taking off her blouse, heard her slapping at the wasps. "Move away," Samara said. "Move away from the nest."

"Go away," Raisa said.

"Me?" Samara asked.

"Yuri. He'll get a bite. It's dangerous."

"I'll take care of her, Yuri. You go up and look after Marty for me."

"Go! Go," Raisa pleaded.

Yuri began to walk backwards along the shore, his eyes full of fear and sorrow.

"Don't worry. I'll look after her," Samara said. She continued to hear slapping noises, and then, "My hair, my hair. Another one in my hair."

Samara turned. Raisa had moved towards the ocean. Samara rushed to her and began to look through her hair, found two wasps, and picked them out.

"Let's get away from here," she said, taking Raisa's hand and leading her down the beach. Out of danger, Samara took Raisa's blouse and inspected it to make sure there were no wasps lurking in it. Then she held it up for Raisa to put on. Only then did she see. Her heart jumped, bile rose in her throat. Raisa's back and arms were covered with scars, small, round alabaster-white scars, made even whiter in contrast to the reddening wasp stings. Samara helped Raisa into the blouse, stepped around to her front to button it for her. Raisa's chest was also covered with the scars, white and glistening, like circles of styrofoam, Samara thought.

"We'd better get you to a doctor," Samara said. "You might be allergic too."

"No, I don't think so."

"It might run in the family; maybe Marty would know."

"He's not my biological brother," Raisa said.

"Oh, O.K. But maybe my mother could call the doctor and see what he says."

"We must make sure Yuri wasn't also stung. Perhaps he was only being brave."

"Yes. Yes. Good idea."

Samara took Raisa's hand, and they walked along the beach. She boosted Raisa over the bank, and Raisa gave her hand to Samara to help pull her up.

"You know now about the scars. I beg of you not to tell. Not to tell any other person. Please, I beg of you. Keep my secret."

"Of course. Wild horses won't drag it out of me. You have my word." Samara reached out and took Raisa in her arms and hugged her. "My God, life is an awful thing," Samara whispered.

"Life is a battle, yes. A fight against evil. You must always be on the side of good, Samara. You must never rest."

"You must never rest." Those words and the image of the scars were present in Samara's mind as she awoke at daybreak. It was already raining, a welcome end to the heat wave. She put on her red poncho and red rubber boots and went out to walk the shore. When she got to the mouth of the river, she turned to walk up its bank, squishing through the mud. Some men were stowing equipment aboard the Sandra D., a boat that took people deep-sea fishing. They were older men, but Samara realized that they had slackened their efforts in order to observe her. Near the road she pulled herself up onto a dock, but instead of walking back by way of the road, she cut through the alders and headed home cross-country. The admiration of the fishermen had raised her spirits, and the feel of the rain on her face continued to dispel her gloom. Nevertheless, Raisa's scars and her words remained present in Samara's mind. As usual, she would meet them at breakfast. But this time there would be something between them, a deeper, more compelling connection.

When she broke through the bushes into the parking lot next to the farmhouse, she saw Raisa and Yuri, hand in hand, coming up from the beach. She waited for them, and the three went into the dining room. As they shed their rain gear, they could smell coffee brewing and even above that the odour of oranges. The whir of the juicer and the bubbling of the coffee urn were jolly sounds.

As soon as they were sitting, Yuri reached across the table and took Samara's hands. "You are a brave girl. You have courage. Not foolish bravado, but true courage."

"Thank you. That's nice of you to say. I'm awfully glad you're feeling well, Raisa."

"The baking soda poultices worked wonders," Yuri said.

"Yuri stayed up all night and kept putting on fresh paste."

"It was nothing. It was the least I could do." Yuri let go of Samara's hands and patted Raisa's cheek. "Right here at this table are two of the children of light. I am very privileged to be eating my breakfast in your company. Raisa and I have been observing you, and even before last night's crisis we were impressed, weren't we, Raisa?"

She nodded. "You are so kind to Marty. And you are a good daughter, we see that."

Samara grinned shyly. "You're going to make me have a swelled head."

"Yes. I must stop. Hubris will enter your soul and your parents will condemn me." He smiled. A crisis had passed, and Yuri was nearly giddy with relief and happiness. "More coffee? Let me be the one to get it this time. To do honour to two incomparable ladies."

As he was fussing with the coffee, Raisa said softly, "You will remember not to mention ... what you saw?"

"You can trust me. To tell you the truth, I don't even know what it was I saw. I mean, I know what I saw but ... "

"But you don't know the explanation?"

"The explanation. Yes. The cause."

"Cigarettes. Lighted cigarettes."

This morning Yuri and Raisa waited for Samara to finish; their habit had been to eat quickly and excuse themselves. They walked with her to the barn and during the morning activities they stood one on each side of her. That meant that Marty's usual place, on Samara's right, was usurped and so Ron wheeled her next to Raisa. And Stevie, who usually stood on Samara's left, had to stand next to Yuri, Sophie on her left.

Carol, commenting later to Samara on the arrangement,

said, "You seem to have become the chief of a clan. The seven of you in a line facing the rest of us."

Samara knew her mother was pleased.

Ron asked Yuri and Raisa to go with Samara and him to the movies Saturday. Stevie would stay with Marty. Sophie was going with her parents to visit friends.

"We don't go out evenings," Yuri said. Raisa looked at him. She wants to go, thought Samara. An hour later, Yuri came to Samara's cabin. "We have changed our minds. We would like to go with you. We have decided that Ron would not take us to a dangerous section of the city. And he will be a careful driver, we think."

The movie was the kind of lighthearted comedy that thoroughly refreshes. When it was over, Ron proposed going to a restaurant. There, both Yuri and Raisa seemed transformed. They were full of life and very funny, taking turns playing straightman for the other in a way that suggested they'd had lots of practice. Ron did his imitations of the other inhabitants of Summerland, a kindly mimicking. He had caught Carol's enthusiasm and Conway's slightly haughty manner; he had Sophie's giggliness and Stevie's otherworldliness.

"My goodness. It's twelve forty-five," Samara said. "They'll be thinking we've eloped."

"Twelve forty-five. That is the latest we have ever been out, isn't it, Yuri?"

"Yes. This Samara is corrupting us." And Yuri laughed, his deep chuckle.

At the farmhouse, Raisa said, "This has been the nicest evening we can remember. We will speak often of it, won't we."

"Yes. It will be an important milestone."

As Ron and Samara were walking down to their cabins, Ron said, "That's a weird relationship. Have you been able to make it out? They don't act like brother and sister at all."

"It's strange all right. A real mystery."

When Samara, Sophie, and Stevie were little, seven to ten or eleven, they would be taken every couple of weeks to the Newcastle library to pick out books, and over those summers each of them read the entire Nancy Drew series as well as the Hardy Boys, and the favourite, the eight volumes of Kate Dandy, Private Detective.

They'd each created their own persona, building and refining it each summer. What would Samara Bellmont, Secret Agent, nine years old, tough as nails and amazing in her ability to use technology, have made of the Raisa-Yuri mystery? Would she have even noticed anything? Yes, probably, because she was a knowing, wise child who took in everything and mulled it over. Back then she had certainly noticed that the Oriental lady had set her cap for her father, and she'd wanted to warn her mother but didn't know what to say. So all that summer (for the lady, Kit-Yin was her name, had stayed all summer even though she'd only registered for two weeks), Samara, Stevie, and Sophie had tailed her. They'd even sneaked Penny's master key and gone into her room in the farmhouse. They'd opened drawers and closet but hadn't dared touch anything else. Sophie had never told her mother. Kit-Yin had a green and yellow parrot in a cage; the parrot looked so real that they'd decided it once had been alive and was now stuffed. There was even seed on the bottom of the cage and a dish of water. Stevie reported Paul's remark to Nita about Kit-Yin, "There's nothing so pitiful as an aging whore."

A letter came from Roger, touching in its inarticulateness, expressive nonetheless of his hurt at being so ignored.

Samara piled her lunch on a plastic plate and went off with it and her writing paper to her cove.

Dear Roger,

    I think of you often.

She crumpled that sheet of paper and began again:

Dear Roger,

    I think of you all the time. I suppose I haven't written because I'm so confused myself that I dreaded having to write things down and then see just how confused I really am. Somehow I've got sucked into the usual activities in spite of my vowing not to.

    I was getting along fine the first couple of days when this couple appeared. She is in a wheelchair and can hardly speak. She has a terrible progressive nerve disease. She's a world famous physicist-mathematician. He is her caretaker. Without really wanting to, I got drawn into helping her. Now I'm almost as much her caretaker as he is. This makes it sound like I'm doing it against my will, but that's not true. At first I pitied her but now I just admire her so much. And, like a miracle, I began to understand her right away. Now three weeks later, I am still the only one who can understand her — me and her caretaker, whose name by the way is Ron. Hers is Marty (short for Martha). Up until now he has had to do everything for her, all the most intimate personal things. But I've sort of taken that part over. I give her a bath, even wash her private parts.

    My mother and father, as you can imagine, are very happy that I'm not sulking around but have found something worthwhile to do. And since I go with Marty (and her caretaker) everywhere, I wind up participating in the stupid activities.

*Nearly everyone is here now. Uncle Philip
came two weeks ago. My strange half-brother is
here with his two children (his wife got them
settled and then just up and left). He is like a
child himself. Uncle Paul hasn't shown up yet.
He's supposed to come this week.*

Writing the letter, Samara alternated between remembering
the last four weeks, daydreaming about Roger, and writing
long detailed descriptions of the guests and events. It was
only when she came to the end and tried to formulate an
expression of her love and her eagerness for his visit that
she had to acknowledge to herself that the most
extravagant protestations, which only four weeks ago were
sincere, would now be hypocritical.

Both Ron and Marty had taken off their watches, part
of Marty's plan for the summer to disregard public time,
since she could not conform to it. Samara had discarded
her watch too, given up listening to the news on the radio,
and stopped reading the newspaper. It was, thought her
mother and father, a wonderful experiment. So today
everyone at Summerland was going to put away his watch
and for one week Rose would call them to meals by
sounding the Chinese gong.

Now Samara could not even guess at the time. She could
stay and try to end the letter truthfully, or she could let it
wait until bedtime. It wouldn't make much difference if
she missed the afternoon activity.

What were they all doing now, she thought.

She gathered up the remains of her lunch, ordered the
sheets of her letter, and waded out into the ocean to round
the point. Every time she made that passage, she
remembered, if only for a second, the time she had cut her
foot on a rock, how astonished she was at the
instantaneous dyeing of the salt water.

She noticed a new car parked in the driveway, not

parked higgledy-piggledy as a tradesman would park it, but neatly stowed for the duration. It must be Uncle Paul's. On this warm day all the doors of the barn were open, so it was easy for her to slip in. Across the circle, Stevie and Nita were nestled on either side of Paul. At intervals he would smile lovingly at one and then the other, pat Stevie's hand, stroke Nita's hair. These were, she knew, perplexing actions to the rest; did he indeed really love the two women and how could they love him?

It occurred to her that she mustn't miss tonight's session; her mother would surely call for storytime and Paul would just as surely answer the call.

It was only two weeks past the longest day of the year, so that when Paul started his story, it was still fully light. The sun was low on the western horizon when he finished, the sky a handsome mauve and gold, illuminating the barn interior with the eerie light of northernness. Paul was, as always, a spellbinding storyteller, but what of his story was true, and what pure fiction, no one could say.

"I've spent the last three months on Quadra Island, in British Columbia, at the Christian Sufi tekne. The Sheik there is ninety years old, still with a very sharp mind, with the body of a fifty year old, and of course the accumulated wisdom of ninety years spent in seeking," he began.

The next day, after the afternoon session, Ron was going into town for supplies. Marty had been planning to go with him, but she began to feel the heat of the day. Samara offered to take her down to the ocean. They would set up under the trees near the river mouth and thus have both shade and ocean breeze. Samara heard Sophie ask Ron if she could go with him — she too had some things to buy. Samara was surprised to feel a twinge of jealousy. She wondered if Marty had felt it too.

Stevie wanted to stay with her mother and father. It was Philip who offered to help maneuver Marty's wheelchair over the bank. "I'll be back in an hour to see if you've had enough fresh air," he said.

"This weather makes me feel so logy," Samara said.

"It gives me rashes, worse than usual."

They sat comfortably in silence.

"Do you wish you had gone with Ron?" Marty said, after a few minutes.

"No, it's too hot."

"But not too hot for Sophie."

Samara smiled. "No, I think she has a crush on him."

"And not you?"

"I don't know. I already have a boyfriend. What about you? I suppose it would be more than a crush for you."

"Of course I love him. But what kind of love is it? That's the important question. What he feels for me is not the love of a man for a woman, I'm reconciled to that. It's really a kind of adoration he feels for me. I think he likes you. Whether as just a friend, I don't know. But he's always so full of life when you're around."

"Maybe. But you're the love of his life, anyone can see that."

Marty chuckled, a sound like the melancholy cooing of a mourning dove.

On Thursday, sleep-in and brunch day, Samara brought her roll and thermos of coffee to the beach. Fred came walking along the shore and sat down beside her. "We must share a gene," he said, "for liking to get up early."

"That's right. Odd, isn't it?"

"Have you always been like that?"

"Yes, always. Much to my mother's sorrow. And you?"

"Always. In fact when I was a teen, I'd get up at four and wander through the woods in back of our house. It was almost as if I could see in the dark — I never got lost. But after I married, I tried to change my habits. So now I wake up at five-thirty or six. In the winter I sometimes stay in bed as late as seven."

They sat together in silence, mesmerized by the gentle surf. Then Fred got up quickly, sucking in his breath.

"God," he said, "oh God."

Samara arose, and he took her hand in both of his, wringing all three. The colour had drained from his face, and his eyes became glassy, as if he were having a seizure.

"No, no, no, no," he said rhythmically.

"Should I call Dad? Are you sick?"

"No, no, no, no," he repeated.

Samara could see him relaxing gradually, his hands slowed down their wringing, he breathed more slowly. Finally he dropped her hand.

"I had one of my sights," he said. "Gina was here, no, over there." He pointed to the rocky part of the shore. "There's blood everywhere."

Samara put her arm around his trembling shoulder. "We'll watch her every minute. Or maybe forbid her to come here."

"It will happen. It will happen."

"What exactly did you see?"

"The rocks. They went forward, wet, dry, wet, dry, and then there was blood, and I know it must have been Gina's blood."

"But you didn't see Gina?"

"No, just the rocks."

The next day, Fred went to bed with a sick headache. Samara heard Carol call the babysitter. She said, "Call her back and cancel. I want to watch them myself."

"O.K., if you say so, but it's not necessary."

In the morning Samara took them to town, played games with them, and then took them on a picnic. But at last Gus said, "It's too hot. I want to go swimming."

On the beach Samara kept noticing her own strange breathing. "God, I'm going to hyperventilate if I keep this up." She tried consciously to regulate her breathing, but that only made it worse.

Gus ran in and out of the water, but Gina seemed

content to stay close to Samara. They went into the water hand in hand.

Gus ran to the rocks. "Be careful," Samara called.

"I will."

Gina and Samara walked to the edge of the rocks. After a few minutes Gus hollered, "Come see this. Come see this funny thing."

Gina let go of Samara's hand and began quickly to climb the rocks. Samara went after her. "Be careful! Slow down," she called. But Gina was scampering along, not seeming to notice the sharp rocks on her feet, as she leapt from boulder to boulder. Samara tripped, scraping her knee. "Wait for me," she called. Gina slowed and looked back.

"You've hurt your leg."

"Just a little. But wait up for me."

Damn, she thought, this is awful. I'm never going to have kids.

When they got to where Gus was standing over a pool in the rocks, Samara saw him poking a crab with a stick. "Don't hurt it," she said. "It's got feelings too, you know, just like you."

"No," he said. "It's not like me. It's like a rock. Come feel."

Samara sat down and tried to will her legs to stop trembling and her heart to stop writhing in her chest.

"Let's go home and have some popsicles," she said. "Carol has made some special kind of popsicles."

For the next two days, Samara did not let Gina out of her sight.

It began to rain Monday morning and rained all day, blowing and cold. Samara felt an immense relief, and after breakfast, an unnatural exhaustion overcame her.

"I'm going to take a nap," she told her mother.

"Are you feeling all right? You look so pale. Do you think you're coming down with something?"

"No, maybe it's just this low pressure system. The wind always makes me sleepy."

She fell asleep immediately and slept through dinner. Carol and Conway took turns going to the dining room. They didn't want to wake her by going into her room, but they also wanted to know if she had a fever. She did finally awake about eight, still feeling exhausted. She ate her dinner in bed, Conway and Carol watching nervously.

She did not dare ask if it had stopped raining. One part of her wanted to ask her mother to open the curtains, the other part dreaded to see the sun. She should get up to bathe Marty — it had been several days since Marty had had a bath — three or four. Her rashes would come back. She couldn't continue to neglect Marty. This accident with Gina could happen years from now. Carol went to get the thermometer. When she came back she said, "The sun is trying to come out. I'll open the curtains."

Samara's limbs became heavy. She could hardly move her legs, could hardly raise the glass to her lips. "Gina. Is Gina on the beach?"

Conway understood at once. "You don't need to take her temperature. I'll go down to the beach and watch. You just rest."

"And Marty. I should give her a bath tonight."

"Ron can give her a bath. What if you are coming down with something? You wouldn't want to give it to her."

"You're right."

"Would you like me to read to you?"

"That would be wonderful."

"There's a fascinating article in the new *Atlantic Monthly* about a man's search for his long lost brother."

"Perfect."

Later, when Samara fell asleep, Conway went over to Penny's and Philip's. It was time for an outing, he and Carol had decided.

When they started Summerland, twenty-four years ago, they had tried to run it democratically with decisions made by the regular and temporary guests alike. That had resulted in long fruitless meetings. Then they'd run it with the regulars making decisions. But Paul was always on the opposite side from the majority, and wrangling occupied a large part of their summer. He had been away a lot the last few years, and so they had got out of the habit of consulting him. Nita was always swayed by the majority unless Paul was there. More and more, an informal visit among Penny, Philip, Conway and Carol resolved issues quickly.

So it was that a few minutes later Conway was back. "They think it's a good idea."

In the morning Carol made the reservations. She was particularly pleased that she could hire a bus equipped for the handicapped so that Marty and Ron could travel with them. And at the evening session, Penny announced the surprise.

Another Place

5

The Maritime Art Heart had been created when two of the area's best known painters died within weeks of each other. Each of them, unbeknownst to the other, had left a bequest to establish an art center. One of them had lived in Wolfville, Nova Scotia, the other in Sackville, New Brunswick. The Tantramar site was chosen because it was central — three hours from Halifax, three hours from Fredericton, thirty minutes from the Prince Edward Island bridge, and close to the ocean. Conway's donation seven years ago, when the Centre had been built, assured Summerland guests a warm welcome each year.

The building, of lightweight plastic and foam, looking like a Japanese house up on stilts, floated over the marshes. On the day the Summerland group arrived, large panels were open and a soft wind blew through the main building. After eleven months of solitude in their own home studios, the artists had gathered here to talk, and everywhere there were small groups in earnest discussion, or in playful banter.

Several walls in the building were designated for temporary murals. Conway and Samara stood in front of one that was a collage of product labels, packaging, and

letters cut from magazines, spelling "THE THIRD MILLENNIUM,
THE AGE OF AQUARIUS, THE ELEVENTH SIGN OF THE ZODIAC,
HAS BEGUN."

The stipulation of the centre's funding was that every
artist, writer, musician, composer, and craftsman in the
Maritimes could have a four-week visit every three years.
Each could, if he wished, use the time as a retreat, but
could also, as most did, use the period as a way to get
fired up. In its short life, the Art Heart had created a
coherent community of artists in the Maritimes. The
centre's influence was not only felt in the art of the region,
but was beginning to be felt in the politics, education, and
general culture.

The Summerland group also insured its welcome by
giving lectures and workshops. For this trip Philip would
demonstrate the use of the computer to figure out
complicated perspective problems in painting. Conway
demonstrated the use of acupuncture to stimulate the
brain's story-telling function. And Paul would teach the
dances of the Mehlevi Sufis.

Gus and Gina happily ensconced in the daycare centre,
Samara and Fred could relax. There were, they could see,
no rocks, no beach.

Before lunchtime of their second day, Yuri asked Carol
if they would like him to give a workshop that afternoon.
Carol, surprised, said yes, and then worried that Yuri
would somehow embarrass them. She arranged to have his
workshop announced with the notices in the cafeteria, and
she found space.

A prickle of anticipation went through Samara as they
gathered — anticipation and apprehension both. Yuri was
even more unpredictable than Paul, whose eccentricity was
somehow second-hand. Marty had planned to take a nap
to prepare her for the ride back to Summerland, but she
couldn't miss this, she told Samara.

Twelve of the resident artists gathered with the entire
Summerland group. Yuri began, "I will call this activity

'Winterland.' There are twenty-six people here. Raisa and I will not participate. We will direct. I will divide you arbitrarily into eight groups of three.

"One of you in each group will be the villain. You can chose any way to decide that — elect, call numbers, volunteer. When you have settled this, I am going to come to each group and give you an assignment."

After the groups had indicated they'd chosen a villain, Yuri went to each. "You," he said, "are group number one. You are going to present to the whole assembly a two-minute dramatization of the Three Little Pigs. One of you knows the story? Fine. You'll have about ten minutes to prepare."

Group two got Gingerbread Man, group three Red Riding Hood, group four Snow White, group five Black Beauty being beaten by his cruel master, group six the horror movie *Maddog*, group seven the man in the news who had kidnapped two children and kept them in a small cell in his basement, making them perform dreadful sexual acts, group eight a scene in Belsen between Jewish children and a German guard.

When the ten minutes were up, Yuri called group one to the front. Philip had been chosen to be the wolf, and Stevie and another woman, a weaver, were the pigs. The weaver played the first two pigs, eaten up, and Stevie played the pig building the brick house. They played with great gusto; the audience laughed and clapped vigorously at the end.

For Red Riding Hood, Paul was the grandmother, Carol the little girl, and a petite Englishwoman, a printmaker, the wolf.

For Black Beauty, Marty played the horse, and a huge man, a poet, the wicked owner. He proved to be a fine actor; his cruelty and anger were palpable. Marty's whinnying was uncanny. It was Fred who rushed in to prevent further beating.

Samara watched the audience. They had been laughing, but now they looked tense. She couldn't tell if Marty wanted to be funny or sad, but she was distressed by the sound. Yuri must have misunderstood the purpose of their coming here — to cheer everyone up. She wondered what her mother was thinking. She could see only half her face.

Samara and a young dancer were the two kidnapped victims. Ron was the kidnapper. In ten minutes they had not had time even to decide how they could possibly dramatize such an unspeakable situation. The dancer had finally suggested they perform a dance which would only suggest such acts. Ron was uncomfortable; he had never acted before, he said, and this role was too dreadful even to imagine. Samara and the dancer writhed and moaned, while Ron stood looking dismayed, twice gyrating his hips, and three times trying to grab the flitting girls.

Samara looked out at the gathering. Once again she couldn't tell what their reaction was; their expressions seemed to her to be ones not of horror or sadness but of discomfort and perplexity.

"Do you know who we are?" she asked.

"Satyr, with Grecian women?" Penny said.

"No."

Carol said, "David dancing naked before the ark of the covenant?"

"No. I don't think we could do this so you could guess, even if we had all day. It's too horrible."

Fred said, "The Harriman kidnapping."

"Yes! How did you guess?"

"I don't know. I just had a feeling that was it."

Nita and a young girl, a short story writer, played the Jewish children. A man named Goldberg, short, fat, played the German guard. He imitated a stage German accent, shoved and pushed the girls toward an imaginary door.

At the end of the scene, there was polite applause. Samara noticed that the people from the Heart got up and left quickly.

Marty, totally exhausted by the trip, went to bed as soon as she arrived back. Samara, also exhausted, nevertheless brought Marty and Ron a tray of supper from the dining room, Sophie trailing along behind with pitchers of milk and water.

"You won't be missing anything. They've canceled our evening meeting. Everyone is too tired. And it's so hot. Even in the barn."

Samara guessed that Marty would like total quiet, so she and Sophie left soon and walked down to the rocky shore by the grotto, where it was always cool.

"Did you hear? About Nita and Paul?" Sophie said.

"No, what?"

"They think they'll not be back here next summer."

"Why?"

"I didn't get the whole story. My mother will probably tell me tonight. But Paul has found another place — he wants them all to move to British Columbia. I guess they are going to go."

"Stevie too? In the middle of university?"

"I guess so. I haven't talked to her since I heard."

A little while later, they saw Stevie wading through the water around the point from Richards' cove.

"I bet she was looking for you," Sophie said.

Samara rose and waved her arms.

When Stevie came up to them, she said, "Those Richards have got a terrible dog."

"It belongs to someone visiting them," Samara said. "He didn't bite you?"

"No, but it scared me half to death."

They sat on the rocks, picking up pebbles and tossing them into the sea.

Finally Stevie said, "So I suppose you've heard the news."

"Sophie just told me. Will you go too?"

"I don't know. I hate to. But my mother will be so torn if I don't. Papa says I can go to the University of Victoria. He says I'll love it."

"Will it be hard to transfer credits?"

"I guess not. Anyway, you're not coming back next summer either, and it wouldn't be the same without you, would it, Sophie?"

"With both of you gone, no. But maybe it's time for a change here. Twenty years is a long time for something like this to last, my mother said."

"If this is our last summer here, I'll never get out of debt. I owe three million," Stevie said.

"What we ought to do is have one marathon game — all night — for high stakes, and give you a chance to get in the black," Samara said.

"Or dig my grave deeper."

"Speaking of digging a grave deeper, I'd better go write Roger. He's quite annoyed at how few letters I've written, especially since I made such big promises of two a day."

For Samara one of the high points of every summer was the camping trip that Paul led to a remote area of Pieuchibouguac Park. At the mouth of the Saint-Luc River, they pitched tents, made campfires, cooked bannock and hotdogs, toasted marshmallows, watched the gray seals playing. Paul was an adept woodsman, and he had taught Samara, Stevie, and Sophie to be competent survivalists.

This year none of the guests wanted to go. Of course Marty couldn't go, Fred was afraid of the dark, Yuri and Raisa were too timid. Conway said his bones were too creaky for a bedroll, Penny felt she couldn't leave the administration, Carol thought she should stay to help. The camping group this year would be smaller with only Nita, Paul, Philip and the three daughters.

Four days before the trip, Samara was staying with Marty after lunch while Ron drove to Moncton for medical supplies. Marty said, "I wish Ron could go tenting. I can tell he would love to go. He's very transparent to me. He says he doesn't really want to go, and then when you all talk about it, he brightens up. He's never been camping. I said we could try. We could always come back here if it didn't go well. I could sleep in the van."

"I'm afraid that wouldn't work. You have to hike in — there's no cars allowed. And no vans or campers for sure."

"I didn't know."

"It's supposed to be primitive camping. There's a pump and a privy — that's all."

"That is primitive."

In the afternoon during quiet time, Samara said to her mother, "I think I should stay here instead of going tenting."

"Why? You love it so."

"I've been thinking. I don't want you to think I'm getting a swelled head, but the others do depend on me — Raisa and Fred and Marty. I hate to leave Gina and Gus. I mean, I know I'm not indispensable, but, really, I think I've become the one they turn to. That might sound silly — you'd be a better one to consult, but it's just happened that way. And another thing is that Marty says Ron would love to go on the trip. She can tell he would, even though he says he doesn't care. If I didn't go, I could stay with Marty and Ron could go."

Carol felt her heart swell, her body warm at this plain evidence of Samara's growing up, of her compassion and thoughtfulness, pleasing her as nothing else could have.

Sunday was a day of rest at Summerland. Some people went into town to go to church. Some people went off by themselves to meditate. It was not uncommon for several to get together to explore the countryside. The Fredericton contingent might visit their relatives. There was no breakfast served, only a brunch at ten. Penny, Philip and

Sophie, when they didn't go to Fredericton, would often go to a nice restaurant for breakfast. Carol often found a spot to be alone. Samara usually didn't see Nita, Paul and Stevie until nearly the end of brunch, twelve-thirty.

At eleven she was sitting on the deck writing a letter to Roger when she saw Gus and Gina going toward the beach. They had been forbidden to go by themselves, Samara knew. Where was Fred? Probably coming along in a minute. Or maybe in his bed with one of his debilitating migraine headaches. Samara waited for a few minutes, but Fred did not come into view.

She stowed her letter under the dictionary and went in the direction of the children.

Maybe they think this is a bit of an adventure, Samara thought when she spotted them walking along the beach. I'll just keep them in view but not let them know they're being watched.

She could see them without going down to the beach, but near the river mouth, the trees were getting in her line of vision, so she scrambled down onto the rocks. The children stopped every few feet to pick up something, maybe smooth rocks or a pretty shell.

Then she could hear Fred's hysterical shouting, "Gus! Gina!"

They heard too, and turned, seeing Samara for the first time.

"Hi," she said. "I think your dad is looking for you."

They didn't look disappointed or guilty, they merely smiled and began walking a little more quickly toward her. She took each by the hand and together they began to jog down the shore toward his voice.

"We're here," Samara called. "Safe and sound."

"Gina! Gus!" By now his voice had become a screech.

"Here, Fred. Here they are."

But then he saw them, and he began to run. He seemed to be in pyjamas and slippers, hobbling from one rock to another. They saw him fall, flat on his face.

"Daddy, Daddy," Gina yelled. Samara let go of their hands and sprinted toward Fred.

"Are you all right?" He lifted his head up; blood was streaming down his face from a cut over his eye. "Oh my God, look at you, Fred," Samara said.

"Daddy! Daddy!" Gina was shrieking.

He got to his knees and put his hand to his forehead. "I can see," he said. "It's not my eye. I can see."

Gina was running.

"Careful. Be careful. The rocks are slippery," Samara said.

But nimbly Gina skipped from rock to rock and threw herself into her father's arms. "It's bleeding. Your face is bleeding."

"It's O.K., poogums. I'm O.K."

Gina pulled off her T-shirt and held it to her father's forehead.

"That's good, poogums. That's a good idea." He started to get up. "Ooo, I'm all woozy," he said.

"You'll need stitches probably. We'd better get you to the emergency ward. Sit here. I'll get someone. Stay right here with your daddy."

When she came back with Ron, Fred was crying. "This is it," he said. And he half-laughed, half-sobbed. "This is it. Gina on the rocks, and blood on her shirt."

My prayers, Samara thought, how strangely they were answered.

Conway drove Fred to the emergency ward while Samara stayed with the children. After brunch, they were going to go for a walk to town to buy postcards, but the sky became lowering and the raindrops began to fall. Soon it was pelting. Sitting at the glass door watching the rain over the ocean, the children were at first exhilarated and then became apprehensive as thunder began to sound.

"Where's Daddy? He should be here," Gina said.

"Sometimes there's a long wait at the hospital. Especially on Sunday." But she herself was worried; five hours

seemed like a long time. When Conway arrived back by
himself, Gina rushed out in the rain. "Daddy, Daddy." But
the doctors had decided to keep Fred overnight; he'd had,
they were afraid, a slight concussion.

"I think," Conway said, "that Fred's brain is such an
unusual one that they couldn't quite make him out. I think
he's going to be fine."

That evening, Penny brought clean sheets so that Samara
could sleep in Fred's bed. When Penny pulled back the
covers, the sheets looked as if they'd not been slept in.

"Are you going to sleep in this bed?" Gus asked.

"Yes, in your daddy's bed," Samara said.

"Daddy doesn't sleep here," Gus said. "He sleeps in our
room."

"Your room?"

"On the floor."

"Isn't this bed comfortable?"

"I don't know. Daddy didn't want to sleep there after
Mommy sang her swan song. He's afraid of the dark."

"Oh," Samara said.

As she was tucking in the sheet, she looked across the
bed to Penny, who was trying hard not to smile.

"There's nothing to be afraid of, Mommy says. But we
have to take care of Daddy, Mommy says. Because Daddy
had a peculiar upbringing."

"Peculiar?"

"That's what Mommy says. My Daddy is a peculiar
man. He is very special so we have to take good care of
him."

"That's very nice of you. Are you afraid of the dark,
Gina?"

Gina did not answer. Gus said, "There's nothing to be
afraid of. But sometimes she's . . . " He looked at Gina.
"She's not afraid, are you? But sometimes when Daddy
screams in his sleep, she . . . I don't know . . . she says, are
you awake, Gus? And I say yes. And she says, Daddy is
having a bad dream. And she says, Can I get in your bed

with you? And I say, yes. We see things on the wall and there are noises. But it is better here than at home. Because when Mommy goes away at home, there are noises on the stairs, and in the basement. Mommy says it's the heating system."

The next day Fred came home, and Samara suggested she stay that night so she could check on him.

He unrolled a futon onto the floor between the children's beds. And at the end of their two beds he set the coffee table on its side, forming a barricade. He brought with him some juice and crackers, a clip-on reading light, a walkman, a jackknife, a flashlight, a note-pad and pen, a barometer, three books, several magazines, and a tiny coffee-maker all ready to plug in, arranged around him on the floor.

In the night Gina woke up Samara. "Daddy is breathing funny."

His breathing did seem irregular and harsh. Samara whispered, "Does he always sleep on his back?"

"I don't know. I can't remember."

"Maybe all these things around him have prevented him from turning over. Could we clear them away?"

"He'd be awfully sad if he woke up and his things were gone."

"I'll just touch him and see if I can get him to turn over."

Samara was relieved that Fred's breathing did indeed seem more normal once he had turned over.

A few minutes later Gina was again at Samara's bedside.

"I can't sleep. I keep hearing Daddy's breathing."

"It's back the way it was?"

"No, but I keep listening."

"Do you want to climb in bed with me?" Samara was surprised to find that Gina's arms and legs were cold. "My goodness. You're like ice." Samara drew her into her arms and was rewarded in a few minutes with a relaxed, warm, sleeping child.

But then of course the discomfort of having a heavy weight on her arms, not being able to turn over herself, the sheer strangeness of the situation prevented Samara from going to sleep. This was a new experience — she'd always been able to go to sleep nearly as soon as her head hit the pillow, even when her nose was stuffed up or she had a stomach ache.

This poor child, she thought. Why has her mother placed such a heavy burden on her. To have to look after your own father. But maybe the mother had to have a relief from the burden herself. Maybe she realized that we all would look out for him. I wonder if he knows he's a burden.

After a while Samara dropped into an uneasy sleep. She was stunned into awakening by a scream, "Gina, Gina."

"Daddy." Samara felt Gina go cold again.

"You stay here. I'll go tell him what happened."

Although it was getting light, it was only five-thirty. Samara persuaded Fred to try to go back to sleep; then she took Gina in her arms again and spoke soothingly. It took longer this time for Gina's thin body to warm and for her to relax, and before she was asleep, Gus appeared. "Daddy is scaring me."

"Scaring you?"

"I'm scared he's going to scream again."

"Is he asleep?"

"I think so."

"Come into bed with us." Samara lay on her back with a child cuddled in each arm. This time it was impossible for her to get back to sleep, even though the children slept. Her arms fell asleep and began to have that peculiar mixture of numbness and shooting pain. She hated to move them, for fear of waking the children, but she knew the time was fast approaching when she could no longer stand to be in that position.

It's strange, she thought, but I've never really felt they were my niece and nephew before. In one night I've grown to love them as much as . . . . She pondered. The quality of this love was different from her love of Roger, who every day seemed more remote. And from that of her love of Sophie and Stevie whom she regarded as her sisters. More like her love of her mother. She and the children were like three parts of a dissected fish, three parts cast into a vast sea, yearning to find each other and become whole again. Samara felt completed. She lay there imagining the three bodies becoming one body, imagining her own strength flowing into the other two.

After a while, she realized that her arms no longer bothered her. They were not numb nor asleep nor in pain. She floated on stillness.

They all slept late; in fact half the camp got up later than usual because of the darkness. In the early morning black clouds had gathered and by eight o'clock the low rumblings of thunder could be heard in the distance.

What woke Samara was a loud clap of thunder and a nearly simultaneous lightning flash. The children woke up too, not knowing what had wakened them. But a second burst of thunder sent each of them burrowing even closer into Samara's side.

"Now you're not afraid of a little thunder," Samara said. There was no reply. "A thunderstorm is one of my favourite things at Summerland. Let's sit up and I'll open the drapes. Then we can see the lightning hit the ocean. It can be the most spectacular sight."

While she was out of bed, Fred cried out, "Oh, oh."

"I'll see what your Daddy wants." She hurried into the other bedroom. He was sitting up on his futon, looking bewildered.

"Where is everyone?" he said. "What is that awful noise?"

"It's just thunder, Fred. Do you want me to open the drapes so you can see the lightning?"

"No, no. Where are the kids?"

"They're in my bed. They got scared. We're watching the storm."

"We certainly were a nuisance to you last night. You must be exhausted."

"Actually, I slept quite well. It's very late — the sky is so dark I woke up late."

"Would you like a cup of coffee?" Fred asked.

"Love one."

"I suppose it's not dangerous to plug this in."

"I don't think so."

"You go back to bed. I'll bring your coffee in to you. Gina can get juice and rolls for us."

In a few minutes, they were all sitting on the bed having breakfast and watching the lightning plunge into the sea. Samara and Gina were sitting against the cushions, and Fred was sitting cross-legged at the foot, with Gus tucked into his legs.

"It's a good thing you guys had juice and rolls because we're going to miss breakfast," Samara said.

When they'd finished their meal, the children went into the living room to play a game. Fred got up to get himself and Samara another cup of coffee, and when he came back, he sat on the bed facing her, his back to the sliding glass door. Samara thought, If anyone comes in, they'll suspect incest.

"I've got to get a hold of myself," Fred began. "It's so hard on my wife, my children. I'd hoped that my father could help. But he seems reluctant to give me advice."

"Would advice help?"

"Doesn't everyone dream of advice so wonderful it will transform him? All those self-help books suggest that."

"I suppose."

"Do you have advice to give me?"

"Me? Good grief. I'm barely able to keep myself in the air."

"But how do you do it? How do you keep yourself in the air?"

"I don't know. I suppose I can because I have only myself to worry about."

Outside the storm was moving away, the thunder growing fainter. They could hear the voices of Gina and Gus. "It's your turn," Gina was saying.

"I wasn't any better when I was single. In fact I was worse, if you can believe that. My wife really helped me. But mostly she comforted me. She couldn't put me on my own feet."

"I'm different from you also because I had such a solid happy childhood. And I don't have your gift."

"Gift?"

"You know. Your seeing things."

"A gift. Good lord."

They were silent a while.

"I think it is a gift though. Really. I mean I think it's a gift from God. Something that singles you out, makes you special."

Fred said nothing.

"Could you maybe experiment? I mean, try for a few days to think of it as a gift. You know we're great ones for experimenting around here."

"But how could that possibly work? A gift. What good could it do for me? What earthly good."

"Maybe that's the wrong way to look on it — what good it can do for you. Maybe it's a different kind of gift. The kind you have to use for others."

Fred was silent again. He looked troubled. The thunder rolled ever more faintly. The children's voices murmured in the living room. The rain splattered on the sliding glass door and drummed on the roof.

And yet there was a stillness and warmth in the room. My brother, Samara thought, the brother I always wanted, turns out to be so strange.

Finally, Fred said, "But what good could it do others? You know it's not the kind of thing that could help me invest. Or even avoid danger."

"Shouldn't you let whoever gave you the gift decide what the gift is good for? Like when my great-aunt gave my mother eight funny forks and my mother had to ask what they were for."

"So who do I ask? Who gave me this? Your father says I inherited it from my great-grandfather. I can't very well ask him."

"Just as an experiment, could you act as if it were a gift from God and ask Him?"

"I don't believe in God."

"But just as an experiment. Act as if there were a god."

"I don't know. I can't see that doing any good."

"Once when I asked my mother why I was so lucky and there were other children so poor, starving and beaten, she said no one knows. That's the biggest mystery of all. But she knew one thing true about that injustice. 'To whom much is given of him much will be required.'"

"'To whom much is given, of him much will be required.' It's true I've been given much. Even if you don't count my so-called gift."

"If we're going to make it to morning activities, I think we'd better get a move on."

"What time is it?"

"Ten."

"Good heavens. We're late already. I won't even have time to shave."

"You can tell them you're growing a beard."

"For my new role as prophet!" Fred laughed at his own joke, and Samara with him.

The evening of the second day of the camping trip, Samara was helping Marty get ready for bed. It had been hot, so Samara suggested a bath to soothe the heat rashes that she inevitably developed. Bathed and anointed with lotion, in her loose gown, Marty reclined in her bed. Samara had opened the sliding glass door wide, letting in the evening breeze from the ocean. Terns were gliding and diving. In quick succession two osprey soared by, both landing on the cedar tree in front of the cabin. The tree jutted out over the bank, and yet the sea wind had shaped it backward, so that it had the appearance of a bonzai tree. The two large birds perching on this battered tree seemed too much, as if the tree would dislodge.

"Can you see them? Let me move the bed." Samara pushed the bed to the left, and propped Marty up higher.

"I can seem them now," she said. "Aren't they magnificent. Like eagles. Not that I've ever seen an eagle either."

"We see the ospreys quite often. But come to think of it, this is the first time I've seen them this summer. One year a pair nested on the Richards' land."

"'They shall mount up on their wings like eagles.' If there were such a thing as reincarnation, I'd like to come back as an osprey."

"I don't know what I'd like to come back as."

Marty answered but Samara did not understand the key word, and had to ask her to repeat it. In fact, Marty had to repeat it twice.

"An arbor vitae?" Samara said. "You'd like to be an arbor vitae? No? Oh, *I* should be an arbor vitae. The cedar tree. Yes. What a good idea. I can just imagine being a tree."

"So strong," Marty said. "So well-rooted to survive storms and battering."

"I'd let you build a nest in my branches."

"I would like that. I would go sailing out over the ocean, but I would always come back and perch on your branch and survey the passing scene."

Samara left the doorway and sat beside Marty, stroking her hair and giving her a gentle hug.

"God made a mistake when He said man and woman had to live together," Samara said. "Men are so much trouble, so hard to deal with."

"I only really know Ron and who could ask for anyone better?"

"Maybe he could be an osprey too, a male one. And you could build a nest in my branches and raise a family of little osprey."

Even after the two birds had flown off, Marty and Samara continued to stare out to sea in silence. At last Marty fell asleep, and Samara extricated her arm from Marty's back. She went into her room, Ron's room, changed into her nightgown, and lay on her bed gazing out to sea. A fishing boat was heading for the river dock, its running lights on, its outlines discernible in the twilight.

There was, she thought, too much to do of the world's work for her to have leisure to spend two more years just studying in college.

She could imagine Marty in her bed, enjoying the three hours' deep sleep that was her reward for expending her energies so generously all day, her breathing becoming ever more quiet until you had to hold your ear to her chest or take her pulse to tell if she were alive.

And yes, why did she have to give up two years of her life, two of the best years everyone told her, to live with no engagement in the real world, only with the world of ideas. She already knew enough to be useful, to look after Marty, or Fred, or Raisa.

Yet, her mother and father were wise, and they did want what was best for her; they wanted her to go back to college.

She thought again of Marty, visualizing her in her bed. She thought of Ron, imagining him around the campfire and knew in her heart that Sophie would be sitting next to him, bending her whole intentions towards pleasing him, amusing him. Roger's face popped into her mind. She thought, I didn't even want to come to Summerland, and I'm hardly here when I'm falling for someone else. Maybe I should write him and tell him not to come.

Before the boat reached the mouth of the river, she was asleep.

An insistent buzz awoke her. A strange noise; what is it? The moon shone full into the room, and Samara knew immediately that she was not in her own bed. Suddenly, her head was crystal clear. Her feet were on the floor. She was running towards Marty's room.

She had closed the drapes after Marty had fallen asleep, so there was no moon to illumine the scene. She could hear gurgling sounds, choking sounds. "Marty, I'm here." For a second she couldn't find the light switch; then a further level of clarity invaded her. She put on the light and saw Marty writhing on the bed, her face contorted; she seemed to be unable to breath. Samara started to say, "What's wrong?" but she stopped on the "what's." Marty obviously could not talk. "Sit her up," came into her mind. "Lift her up." She obeyed the command. A seizure. What had Ron said about a seizure? Keep her calm. Be calm.

Samara sat on the bed and put her arm around Marty's shoulders. She closed her eyes. Centering, she thought. I can do that. I've had enough practice. I can keep calm. She forced herself to breath deeply, thought, God help, said the words to herself over and over, first desperately fast, then forcing herself to repeat them slowly, calmly. She could feel strength and calm and warmth leaving her. More power, she said, Give me more power.

Marty's convulsing began to slow down; she seemed to be catching a breath.

Samara concentrated more. No trance, she said to herself. I can't go too deep. But the concentration seemed to be generating energy, not calming it. She was relaxed but astoundingly alert. And she could no longer tell where her body left off and Marty's began; she was not sitting on the bed or even inhabiting the room — she was of the bed, of the room, she was pure energy, merged into the pure energy of the room, of Marty, of everything. Marty was breathing more easily.

"Stand," Marty finally gasped out. Samara understood immediately, and swung Marty's legs over the side of the bed. She stood up herself and tugged and lifted Marty to a standing position, holding her there under her arms with all the strength she had. She tried to hold Marty's shoulders back at the same time she was holding her upright, so that her lungs could have more air.

The spasms were subsiding, and just when Samara thought she could no longer hold her, Marty said, "Chair." Samara moved her towards the wheelchair, but Marty said, "No," and Samara understood that Marty should be in her fixed chair, the therapeutic chair designed to hold her in the best position. That chair was across the room, and Samara did not know if she could carry her so far. Marty was thin, weighing no more than ninety-five pounds, but she was also nearly dead weight and Samara had her in an awkward grasp.

I should have rung the bell for Dad, she thought. I should try to get her back into the bed and ring the bell. Or chance it to the chair. The words appeared in her mind again, Give me more power. She moved slowly across the room, reached the chair, managed to turn Marty around and lower her into the seat. She adjusted her so that the contours of her body fit the contours of the chair. Then she went into the bathroom and rang the alarm for her father. She sat next to Marty, stroking her arm. Her father and mother were there immediately in pyjamas and bare feet. Samara let them in, and explained in a few words, breathing heavily. Marty gasped out, "Crisis over."

"The crisis is over," Samara translated. She thought, My father's feet are so small and delicate. How can they hold him up?

Carol's heart had jumped at Samara's appearance — her totally white face. "You come and lie down a bit," she said. "Your father will stay with Marty."

Samara reached out and took Carol's hand. She felt that she was about to disintegrate, and she reached out with the other hand for her mother's shoulder. She could not talk, could not even think. Carol half-dragged her to her bed. Her mother kissed her forehead. "You're as cold as a corpse. I'm going to get you some warm milk."

The next day, Samara tried to act like her old self so that Marty would not feel guilty. Carol was not fooled and insisted on staying with them overnight. Marty had a delicate sense of decorum, and she did not mention her discomfort at the amount of trouble she was causing, but she was subdued.

Samara could not explain to herself the extreme weakness she felt. True, she had had to exert herself physically and mentally, but after she had a good night's sleep, shouldn't the exhaustion have gone away? Her mind seemed to be flying off in all directions.

The campers returned in high spirits. Their adventure had been fine, capped by the thrill of having seen two whales cavorting in the bay.

Samara skipped evening activities and went to bed right after supper. She drew the drapes and lay there in the semi-darkness. At first she was too debilitated to pull her thoughts into the suitable organization that was needed for sleep. At last she began to relax, savouring the absence of responsibility. When I get up in the morning, she thought, I'm going to be an entirely new person.

Gradually she drifted off and awoke at 9:30 a.m. after a deep sleep.

She opened her door. "Mom?" she called.

Her mother came out of their bedroom. "Good morning, you sleepyhead."

"I've overslept."

"You needed to."

"Probably."

"You look much better. Not so pale."

"I feel better. I even feel hungry."

"Go back to bed and I'll bring you a banana milkshake and a donut."

Samara opened the drapes. It was a dark gray day, threatening rain. What luck the campers had — sun the whole time and the minute they got back it rained.

It continued to be rainy and cold for two days. The paths became muddy, the barn too cold and damp for comfort. On the third day Samara came down with a cold that left her sneezing and feeling weak, alternately too warm and too chilly.

Marty sent her a message via Ron: I have long ago had to give up the luxury of regretting what I must put my relatives and now my friends through. I must rely on my hope that the extraordinary unselfish acts my friends perform for me strengthen them and make them superior people. I must rely on the hope that they receive their just reward.

At the back of Samara's mind sat the Roger problem and every day brought the problem closer. Two days before his arrival, she decided to go out for a walk. Maybe she just needed some wholesome exercise. Across the main road, not far above the bridge, a brook ran through a meadow and emptied into the river. The brook had for a long time intrigued her — its waters were so clear. She decided to follow it, maybe even to its source.

She asked Rose for a picnic lunch, and packing it and some supplies — matches, her multi-use jackknife, a compass, a small towel, some teabags and a can for boiling water — into a knapsack, she set out, down the shore to the river mouth, up the river bank, under the bridge, and finally to the brook itself. It had been several years since she'd been this far up the river bank — for the past few years the town center with the handsome exotic Acadian teenagers had interested the three girls more than exploring. She was a little disappointed that the water in the brook seemed less pure than she remembered, but even that disappointment did not prevent her spirits from rising as she tramped through the meadow. At the far end of the field, the brook emerged from a spruce and birch woods, its bed becoming rocky as the terrain began to rise. Branches and larger stones made little dams; roots of trees made small caves. The woods were denser and her way impeded by blowdowns. She had set out in cloud, but now she could see streaks of sun filtering their way through the trees, glancing off the surface of the water. Her compass told her that although she had started out going north, she was now headed west. The terrain flattened out again, the woods became birch, and then returned to the dark spruce; "foreboding" was how her father described the New Brunswick spruce forest.

The dead lower limbs of the densely-packed trees scratched at her and made the going difficult. Once she had to swing out away from the brook because it was impossible to get through. In some places the trees were further from the banks, light came in, and at one such spot Samara stopped to examine a delicate green plant with a minty smell. As she was sitting there dangling her hand in the water, an image came to her: a man being hurled from a cliff to his death. She felt the thud of his body.

She pressed on. Abruptly she was there, at the source, a round deep pool. The place was as dark as evening with the spruce coming right down to the edge of the water. The woods here were very still.

She hung her knapsack over the limb of a tree and squatted down beside the pool. It was alive with tadpoles.

A spring must be feeding this, she thought. There was something not quite right, not quite real, about the place. She inhaled an earthy smell and another smell, too, like the odour present just before it rains.

The air thickened; she knew that a presence was there. Her skin crawled. She stood up. The presence was good, she felt, but frightening too, as if a specific personal responsibility was implicit in it.

The water and the tadpoles were transfigured into worthiness.

The presence and the worthiness drained away, reassurance poured into her. She was trembling but peaceful when the mystery had finally faded and hid itself again.

I'm hungry, she thought, but this isn't a good place for a picnic. She went back along the brook, crossed it so that she could take a new way home. She found no safe place to make a fire, so she settled for a soft bed of moss against a spruce tree to have her picnic. The egg salad sandwich tasted wonderful, and even Rose's practice of putting cold french fries in a box lunch seemed like an excellent idea. When she opened the thermos, a rush of a lovely orange smell came at her.

On Thursday afternoon, Samara went to play games with Gina and Gus. The sunny period had been short-lived, and now the rain was sifting down, gently but unendingly. After two hours of play, Samara suggested that she bring over their video machine and play them a movie. When Fred came back from the afternoon activities, Samara and Fred took cups of tea into the bedroom while the children watched the movie.

During a rambling talk, he said, "Fortunately both the kids take after their mother."

Samara said, "By the way, when do you think she will be coming back?"

"Oh that one. I don't think she is."

"I see. You'll meet her in Cleveland, then."

"No, what I mean is that I think she has left us for good."

"Fred, that's awful. Why on earth?"

"We're too much for her. I've had a hunch all along she was hoping that our trip here would mean that she could dump the responsibility on someone else. On Conway, I suppose. And so I wasn't surprised when she left. She saw that there were people to look out for us."

"But poor Gina and Gus. They'll be devastated."

"I don't know. This has been gradual. They're used to being away from her. And she did bring them up to be strong. That took a lot of her will — raising them to be strong."

"How will you cope with them? When you get home, I mean."

"I'm not going home."

"Oh."

"No, I'm never going home."

"Where are you going? Maybe that's a nosy question."

"Not nosy. You have a right to ask. But I don't know. I just know — actually I knew as we were driving away from Cleveland — that I would never see that apartment again."

"You must have felt awful."

"I always feel awful."

"Poor dear Fred."

He began to run his finger around the edge of the cup, round and round, staring at the tea, his head bowed, tears oozing from his eyes.

"How will you make ends meet?"

"I'll have to get a job. I've had some training, you know."

"No, I didn't know. What?"

"I took a medic course. To be an ambulance driver."

"But you don't drive."

"I could learn. I was even thinking of asking Ron to teach me. It would be good to learn on a van like that, don't you think?"

"That would be perfect. And I think he'd be a good teacher."

"That's what I thought. Patient."

"Very patient."

Samara's news was greeted with interest at home. "I thought something seemed funny there," Carol said.

"I've sired a rare bird. That makes me feel even more regret," Conway said.

"But Mom, Dad, you know he could never be an ambulance driver. He can't even manage himself, never mind someone else at death's door."

"That certainly seems to be true. People do rise to occasions, but in this case, I can't see it happening," Carol said.

"She — his wife or his partner or whatever she is — thought we'd look after him. That's clear. You would provide for him."

"And I will, of course. They'll have to have a place to stay and a housekeeper," Conway said.

"Should it be near us?" Samara asked.

"I don't know. We'll have to think that through quite carefully. I certainly don't want his demands ruining your life."

"He is my brother, Daddy."

"I'd be disappointed if you didn't recognize your obligation. But for now, for the next few years, your job is to get an education."

"And he could be wrong. His wife could appear any day and take them all back to Cleveland," Samara said.

"We can hope for that," Carol said.

At breakfast the next morning, Yuri said, "Raisa and I

do not want to pry, but last night your brother told us that his wife would not be returning. Could that be true?"

"It seems strange, doesn't it. But that's what he believes."

"Do you think, then, that it would be acceptable if Raisa and I offered to share the burden with him? Of course Raisa would be in charge. She knows about children a little bit. But I would feel privileged if I too could be of service. Otherwise, we are afraid the burden will fall on you and on your parents. Your parents have much to do already and of course your beau is coming soon."

"Gee, that would be excellent. I know Fred would appreciate it. So would I. And the children need attention. They need to be allowed to play, don't you think? They have to spend so much time just hanging around while the adults talk."

"That's very good news. Raisa and I have been searching for a way that we could contribute our share."

"What do American children that age like to play?" Raisa said.

"I don't know. Maybe go for a walk. Climb a tree. Play hide and seek."

"Cowboys and Indians?"

"Probably. Or spacemen maybe."

7

Friday came and Samara drove into Moncton to meet Roger's plane. Conway let her take his Lagonda instead of the family Volvo, so she felt sporty and sophisticated. She was relieved, in Roger's embrace, to feel some of the passion for him she had felt in the spring. His visit wouldn't be quite as awkward as she had feared. But she also knew that she was seeing him clear-eyed, and what

she saw was a nice young man, quite handsome, with no
depth at all. She let him drive the Lagonda, at least as far
as Pelerin Bridge. He was full of talk about their mutual
friends, and full of anecdotes of his guard duties.

At the beginning of the summer, Carol had suggested
they put Roger in the farmhouse. Samara was upset; she
wanted him to sleep on the hide-a-bed in the living room
of their cottage. But as the time drew closer to his visit,
she'd confessed to her mother that she thought the
farmhouse was a better idea. She'd also informed her
parents that she and Roger would not participate in any
of the activities and would take most of their meals away
from the dining room. But now she changed her mind
about this too. How would she entertain him for eight
days? She wouldn't know what was going on with the
others. She would miss seeing them.

Summerland was in the midst of a crisis when Samara and
Roger returned. Stevie, dusting, had knocked Nita's bottle
of Jacob's Well water from the shelf; the bottle had
smashed. Stevie was horrified at what she'd done, and Nita
was trying very hard to act casual so as not to alarm Stevie
even more. But it was evident to everyone, and of course
to Stevie herself, that this accident was shaking Nita to her
bones. Always Nita's last act, when moving, was to wrap
the bottle carefully and put it in her purse. She would sit
in the car rehearsing whether she'd forgotten anything —
the stove is turned off, the thermostat is down, I've got the
toilet articles, my reading glasses — you've got your
reading glasses, Paul? and the money? and I've got the
bottle of water.

Penny and Carol knew how deeply these superstitions
went with Nita, and they were troubled. Penny was
carefully sweeping up the pieces of mustard bottle, and
Carol was making tea when Roger and Samara arrived.

Nita was kneeling in front of Stevie, saying, "It's all right. Now don't cry. I'm not angry."

"I know you're not angry. You're so wonderful. You never get angry. But I know you're sad."

Paul was standing in the doorway to the kitchen with his hands behind his back, looking troubled, a very unusual expression for him, Samara thought. There was a flurry of greeting when they entered. Stevie and Sophie had been excited because they'd heard so much about the fabulous Roger; they anticipated some drama when he finally arrived, but even his appearance could not console Stevie.

When they all were seated with tea, Paul arose.

"This is, every one of you knows, there's no need to pretend otherwise, a bad blow for Nita, and for Stevie, whose understanding and kindliness is immense. So we must have a solution, a remedy, and I will propose this: that in September the three of us make a pilgrimage to Jacob's Well to bring back our own holy water."

Nita's face lit up. "Could we? Would it be possible? Could we afford it?"

Stevie rushed toward Paul, embracing him. "Papa, what a wonderful idea. You are so smart."

Later, walking along the beach, Roger said, "They're a little muddled, aren't they? All that over a bottle of water?"

"They're a little Mars-bound, I guess. But awfully good-hearted. Uncle Paul is the hardest person to figure out. Sometimes I get so annoyed at how he treats them, and then, like today, he does such a nice thing. My father thinks that everything he does is calculated — that even when he seems to be mean to Nita, he does it for a good reason. And the proof is that Nita has been mentally stable all these years, even though no one could have predicted it. My father watches Paul closely — he says it's one of his most interesting games, to try and figure him out."

"Have they been friends a long time?"

"For years and years."

"This whole place seems a little muddled."

"I'm used to it so maybe I don't notice."

Roger touched her constantly in public — putting his arm around her, holding her hand, burying his face in her hair. She was surprised to find that she was embarrassed and, especially when Ron was present, troubled.

On Monday after the evening activity session, Samara and Roger agreed to babysit while Conway and Fred went for a walk. From the deck they could see the two men standing on the shore looking out to sea. They saw Fred put his hands on his head and double over, saw Conway put his arm around Fred's shoulders and bend toward him. Fred writhed, as if in pain. Conway helped ease him into a sitting position, but he continued to writhe.

"You stay here. I'll go see if they need help. I'll wave if they do, and you get my mother," Samara said.

She ran toward the beach. Philip, too, must have witnessed the scene because he came out of his cabin, moving quickly to the shore. He stopped some yards short. Fred was shivering violently. Samara called, "Uncle Philip, get a blanket."

After they'd put the blanket around Fred, he gradually stopped shivering. His face was chalk white.

He began to gasp out, "I saw, I saw."

"You don't need to talk yet. Just rest," Conway said.

"I saw, I saw, I saw." Then he said, "Pray for me, Samara. Pray out loud."

Samara looked into her father's face, seeking advice. He nodded yes.

She didn't know what to pray for, what words to use, who to address in the prayer. God? Fred didn't believe in any kind of God. Samara didn't know if she did either although she was sure now that there was a mystery at the heart of the world. She began:

You who looks after the world, come to us and stay with

us. We are confused and upset. Help us to overcome confusion, help us to understand our gifts, help us to use the gifts we have been given in the best way. Bring peace and calm and order to my brother Fred. We know the Kingdom of God would like to take up residence in our hearts, but we have to invite it in.

Fred reached out for her hand, taking it between his hands.

"Samara, I'm going to die. You must take Gina and Gus. Your father and mother are too old. I beg of you, tell me you'll look after my children. You are going to be a special woman, with a fine future, but nevertheless, you must make room for Gina and Gus."

"You're going to be all right, Fred. Don't worry. You're not going to die. You're a young man."

"I have seen it. Just now I saw it. And much more I saw." His voice got louder and stronger until he said in a voice like an evangelist's, "The Lord has blessed you."

They all sat or kneeled there in silence. Finally Fred said, "I'll go up to bed." They helped him, still trembling, to his cottage. Conway stayed with him in the living room until he'd undressed. Before he was going to creep into the children's room to his futon, he said, "Could I see Samara before I say goodnight?"

Conway came out onto the deck and whispered, "He wants to see you. Try to keep it calm and brief."

"You must agree, dear sister," Fred said. "I won't be able to sleep for fear I might die in my bed without your consent."

"Of course, Fred. Of course I would look after them."

"You're a good girl." He patted her cheek and then went into the bedroom. Samara kept the door open until she saw him disappear between the two beds. Then she saw, by the nightlight, his arm rise up and wave.

Later on the beach, Roger said, "Are there any normal people around here? Are they all Mars-bound?"

"My parents are normal."

"That's debatable. They're kind of strange. But I suppose they're normal for here."

"Philip and Penny are really normal."

"Yeah, I can see that. I wonder why they hang around here?"

"Because it's interesting. Always something going on."

"You've changed your book. Two months ago, you were saying what a terrible place this was, so boring."

"You're right. But you get drawn into it. And this year, for some strange reason, I'm drawn in more than I ever have been. Just coincidence I guess."

"No one seems to be able to do anything without you. That lady in the wheelchair, those two peculiar ones in the farmhouse. To say nothing of your spooky brother."

"You're not being fair. They really are all very nice. And the lady in the wheelchair, Marty, is internationally respected. She knows the mathematics that explains the whole universe."

"How could you tell? She seems pretty retarded."

"Don't be ludicrous. Retarded. My God. One of the smartest people in the world."

"And what kind of perverted relationship does she have with her keeper? What does he get out of it?"

"Roger! You're disgusting. Ron thinks it's his duty to look after Marty. Because she's so important to science."

"The whole place gives me the creeps. What is all that noise that comes out of the barn? That music from outer space. What are they doing in there?"

"I don't suppose you'd like to see?"

"No thanks. I'm not turned on by queer stuff."

"I think I'd better get to bed. I'm tired."

Samara got up, but Roger continued to sit. She was surprised but relieved that he didn't get up to embrace her.

"Goodnight," she said.

"Yeah," he replied.

She turned around several times on her way to the cabin

to see him still sitting there staring out at the ocean. She undressed in the dark with the drapes open and watched to see when he'd leave. She fell asleep not having seen him go.

He did not come down for breakfast the next morning, so Samara went to the barn for the activities, positioning herself so that she could see him come out of the farmhouse. At ten-thirty he appeared, keeping his head down so that he couldn't catch anyone's eye. He walked up the driveway toward the road. Samara couldn't decide whether to run after him; she was sorry that his vacation was turning out to be so unhappy, but she didn't know how to remedy the situation.

At lunch, Rose said, "Your friend said to tell you he wouldn't be back until after supper. He asked the way to town and to the public beach."

Late that evening Roger knocked on Samara's door. "I've changed my flight. I'm leaving tomorrow. Can someone bring me to the airport?"

"Yes, of course. I'm sorry it's turned out this way."

"So am I. I have a lousy eight days of vacation all year and this is what I get. My flight is at ten-twenty. Goodnight."

After a painful, silent drive to Moncton, Samara returned as morning activities were finishing. Ron pushed Marty's chair toward her as she was getting out of the car.

"Your friend left early?" Marty said.

"Yes. Things didn't work out."

"We're very sorry, aren't we, Ron?"

Ron grinned at Samara over Marty's head.

"Dreadful sorry," he said and lowered his eyes.

Samara went for a walk, along the beach, towards the river mouth. She could hear some low murmuring and when she turned a corner in the path, she saw Raisa and Gina sitting underneath a misshapen spruce tree. Gina was examining the ground; Raisa was examining Gina. Raisa's face was a study in sorrow, not of the moment, but of a lifetime. Her skin seemed thin around her eyes, dark and stretched. There was no colour to her face, yet it seemed illuminated with adoration. Good lord, Samara thought. I hope she's not getting too fond of the child.

When Samara had admired the strange circle of mushrooms Gina had found, they all walked back to Fred's cabin. Gus had invented a game for Fred, Yuri and him to play. They were ships sailing. Each of them was sitting on a pillow and sliding on the floor, bumping into each other because of the imaginary wind or waves. Gus was beside himself with excitement and Fred was laughing hysterically. Yuri looked as if he were trying hard to be festive. Samara was recruited to get three more pillows so that she, Gina and Raisa could play too. Then Raisa discovered that she could push Gina on the pillow, making her go faster. "Me too, me too," Gus cried. So Samara pushed Gus. "Push Fred," Gina commanded. So Yuri pushed Fred, who sang out, "Whee, whoopie."

Later that evening Marty was relaxing in bed after Samara had given her a bath. Ron and Samara were sitting talking to her.

Samara said, "You know, my whole plans for my life have been turned upside down this summer. Now I don't have any idea what I'm going to do."

"University?" Marty said.

"I don't know. Of course my parents want me to finish. But where? And study what?"

"Isn't that what university is supposed to do? Help you plan your life?" Marty said.

"I thought it was to teach you something."

"That too. But most people have no idea what they want to do when they go to college. It's the rare bird who has his goals set at eighteen."

"Why don't you come to the University of Minnesota and live with Marty and me?" Ron said. "Wouldn't that be good, Marty? She could help me translate in your lectures. Maybe she'd get interested in this math and physics you do."

"That would be wonderful. But I'm a wet rag for a twenty-year old to live with. She'd want dates, parties."

"There are men in St. Paul, and parties. Well, it's just a thought."

"I'm touched that you'd ask me." Samara wasn't sure if Marty was happy at the suggestion. But once it had been made, the idea remained ever present in her head. The next day, Ron said, "Marty and I have been talking over my rash invitation, and the more we talk about it, the better it seems. So give it some serious consideration."

"Actually, I have been thinking about it. Could I get into the university so late?"

"Maybe it would be some kind of provisional thing. But Marty is sure she can fix it up — she says students as bright as you deserve special treatment."

"My high school marks were good. And my SAT's were high. Even my college marks aren't too bad."

Samara mulled over the idea. Saturday evening she said to her parents, "Marty and Ron have made me an offer. They asked me to come to St. Paul and go to the university there. I'd stay with them and help Ron in Marty's lectures — translating and putting stuff on the board. I don't know how much good I'd be — I wouldn't understand anything. I don't know what you think of the idea."

"My goodness. This is a surprise. Not a bad surprise. I don't mean that. But unexpected," Carol said.

"I don't know. On the surface of the thing, it sounds like an excellent plan. You'd be in an exciting intellectual environment, you'd have a very good chance to see if science is a field you'd like to pursue," Conway said.

"You wouldn't be disappointed if I don't continue at Tufts?"

"Not at all. These family traditions provide some guidelines when nothing else does. But here is something more interesting. Or at least that's my first reaction. Of course it will take more thought, more discussion. What do you say, Carol?"

"I agree. At first glance, the idea is intriguing. I'm used to your being only a few miles from home. But I'd already warned myself that we shouldn't be running over there every few minutes."

Conway and Carol went for a drive Sunday, and Samara was quite sure they wanted to have some extended time alone to talk over this latest proposition. Her speculation was confirmed when Sunday night the three congregated again in their living room.

"The more we think about it, the better it sounds — this going to St. Paul," Carol began. "To be with two such fine people, to have you in this serious intellectual milieu, seems too good to be true. The only drawback is, will this be too serious? Will you be too strongly influenced to go in a direction that might not be right for you?"

"And would your work for them, for Marty, be too strenuous, interfere with your studies?" Conway said. "But these are things that could be worked out, I think. And if you're aware of the pitfalls, you can avoid them. So, if you're still interested, perhaps we could get the machinery rolling. There are four more weeks until school begins and two more weeks of Summerland. You could always change your mind."

When Samara told Fred about her plans, he said, "Oh dear. I was counting on having your mother and father to help you with Gus and Gina."

Over the next few days, at mealtimes or in the midst of centering in the barn, or sitting in the Bellmonts' living room, Fred would utter what appeared to be an involuntary groan, a cry of anguish.

Was he ill? they questioned. In pain?

"No, no, it's nothing. Please disregard it. It's nothing." And he seemed to be genuinely embarrassed.

Late one evening, nearly midnight, Gina came running

to the Bellmonts in her thin nightdress and bare feet, and knocked on Samara's door. "Come, come," she begged.

Samara threw on her rain coat and ran after Gina. Conway appeared at his door. "What's the matter?"

"Gina's come after me. You come too."

Fred was sitting on his futon, between the children's beds, holding his knees, rocking back and forth, and groaning.

"Fred. What's wrong? Are you sick?"

"No," he moaned.

"What?"

"Samara. In my whole life, I've never had a consolation like all of you." He began to sob, great gulping, tearless sobs. Samara rubbed his back.

"There, there. It'll be all right. It'll be fine. There, there."

Her father was standing in the doorway, his arms around Gina and Gus who both looked alarmed. Samara said, "Take Gina and Gus to mom and have her give them some hot chocolate. Come back." When they'd left, Samara said, "Let's go sit in the living room." As Fred rose, she could see that he'd gone to bed fully clothed, with even his shoes on.

"I can see, I can see, and I'm powerless," Fred gasped out.

"What do you see?"

"My death."

"You're healthy. You're a young man. You aren't going to die." Suddenly Samara thought of suicide. "You're not planning to do it yourself? Cause your own death?"

"No, no, no. But I see it. I see it coming. And what about Gina and Gus — what will become of them?"

Conway came into the room as Samara said, "I told you I'd look after them. I gave you my word."

"But in school? In Marty's house, how could you, it wouldn't be possible."

Conway interrupted, "You're not going to die. Not

soon. But Carol and I would help Samara. We could move
to St. Paul. Supply a housekeeper. Any one of a number of
ways. I give you my word. They will be looked after very
well. After all, you forget, they are my grandchildren. My
gift to the future."

"A few weeks ago you were strangers. And now I have
to put my whole trust in you."

"But surely we'll be able to find their mother. She'll
want to participate in looking after them?"

"She's gone. I knew she would go. I didn't see it. But
still, I knew that one day she'd be gone. She had things to
do — important things to do."

He shuddered and began to rock from side to side,
keening. "Hmmm. Ohhh. Hmmm."

It gradually became an unearthly sound, not a moan or
a lamentation, not a sound of madness or sorrow or fear. It
was, Samara thought, the sound of awe, the sound of a
man who was looking into the heart of things and was
seeing the chaos and inhumanity there. She put her arm
around him, but he continued to rock from side to side.
She, clinging to him as if to a pendulum, began to see
through that sound what her brother was seeing. She was
looking in at the outlines of the power of chaos, the threat
to goodness. Evil was an inadequate word, even a silly
word, to describe what Samara was beginning to see.

Time passed; Fred continued to keen; they both
continued to rock. Conway looked helpless.

The pendulum became shorter; the sound grew fainter.

"Everything's going to be all right," Samara murmured.

"It's going away. You're chasing it away," Fred said. "I
don't feel so cold. I'm not seeing it. It's getting dimmer. I
think it's going away. I knew you were the one who could
drive it away. You have the authority. Your heart is filling
it all in. I can see your heart chasing after it."

At last Conway said, "Why don't we all go back to our
cabin and have something to drink. I'll get your futon,
Fred, and you can sleep with us."

Samara said, "I'll get the kids' pillows and teddy bears."

Carol was sitting on the couch with Gus on her lap and Gina snuggled up against her. "Daddy," Gus said. "We've got marshmallows in our chocolate."

Marty and Ron assured Fred that they would be happy to have Gina and Gus. "Marty's house is huge — now we take in students because it seems to be selfish to keep all that space empty. We made two complete apartments upstairs — usually two or three students share each of them."

Fred seemed reassured. He even became quite jaunty, cracking jokes, and greeting everyone heartily..

One evening, sitting on the Bellmonts' deck, he said, "Now I'm feeling so good that I'm having my doubts."

"Doubts?"

"What if I don't die right away? What if I've made a mistake? Now everything is arranged — the children are going to St. Paul. But what would I do if I don't die?"

Samara, Carol, and Conway weren't thinking of the children's accompanying Samara to St. Paul with that much finality. The idea that he hadn't even thought of an alternative surprised them.

"Won't you go back to Ohio?" Carol said.

"Back to Ohio?"

"To your home there."

"To our apartment?"

"Yes."

"But how would I pay for it? What would I do for money? Goodness. I suppose I would have to get a job. And cooking. Laundry. And the taxes. Who would do the taxes?"

Over the next few days, Fred started to keep a list of things he would need to do if he were to live by himself with the children. This growing list began to overwhelm him, and his greetings became perfunctory again, his face pale.

"You see?" he said, showing the list to Samara. "Who is to buy the children's clothes? If I put money in their hands and sent them into a store, would the clerk help them? Is that ever done?"

"That seems like a pretty good solution to me."

"Do you think so? Really?"

And another day, "See, here? Two new items. Little girls — when do they become — you know — women — all that messy stuff."

"Their periods?"

"Yes, that."

"About twelve, thirteen."

"I'll be dead by that time surely. You'll be able to deal with all that."

At breakfast on Wednesday, he said, "I have a big yellow spot there." He indicated a place six inches in front of his eyes.

"You don't seem worried," Samara said.

"No! It's quite cheerful, actually. A bright yellow spot with some black lines."

Raisa said, "You could be an artist, if you see bright colours like that."

"An artist. I can't even draw a straight line."

The next morning at brunch Raisa asked, "Is your yellow spot back?"

"It is, you know. But this morning it's surrounded by a very beautiful blue. I don't know what you'd call that blue. Wedgewood blue? No, dustier than that. A bit more purply. With a kind of watered silk look."

"So," said Yuri the day after, "how's your spot?"

Samara could tell that Yuri and Raisa were much amused by this spot. Whether they thought Fred was crazy, she couldn't tell.

"Today, would you believe, the spot has changed shape. Instead of just being a blob, it's become a perfect circle, three-dimensional. The center is receding and the beautiful blue is reaching towards me. It's almost as if I could walk right in to the center and keep going until I got to a tiny door down at the end of the tunnel."

Sunday's meal schedule was different, so Samara, Fred, Yuri, Raisa, and the children didn't have breakfast together. But on Monday, Raisa said, "How is our favourite spot this morning?"

"It's become a cone. And the blue has developed little feelers, or maybe they're fingers, moving like those plants underwater do. As if they want to touch me. And the door is hidden now — down at the end of the cone, where I can't see. Maybe it's not even there anymore."

Samara, Conway and Carol discussed the spot, but Fred seemed so cheerful that they hadn't become alarmed. On Tuesday, the fingers of the beautiful blue were actually touching Fred, and they "feel wonderful."

In the night Gina came running for Samara again. "Daddy wants you."

Fred was lying on his futon, his face lit up in ecstasy. "I'm going," he said. "The fingers are coaxing me in. They feel so lovely. Just lovely. The blue is all around me now. The yellow is pulling me in. I'm going to let go pretty soon. It's such a cheerful yellow. It will make me so happy. Gina, dearie, I love you. Look after Gus. Be a good girl for Samara. Gus, make something of yourself. Learn to be useful. Conway, father. Thank you for the gift of life. Samara. You have been a consolation in my last days. You will be a fine woman. Mark my words. A truly powerful human being. I love you. I love you all."

Samara called out, "Don't go, Fred. Hang on!"

"No, it's not possible. They're calling me now. The sound of many waters. The splashing, the echoing. And the smell of raspberries. There must be a patch of raspberries down there. I'll have raspberries and cream when I get there. I'm going now. I'm leaving. Here I go. Goodbye, goodbye. I love ... "

His body went rigid, his eyes staring.

The four stood over him unable to move, dumbfounded.

"Where is he going?" Gina cried. "Daddy, where are you going?"

Gina's voice broke the spell. Conway fell to Fred's side and began to thump on his chest.

"Don't hurt my daddy," Gus yelled. "Don't hit him."

"Shush," Gina said. "He's just waking him up."

But Fred wasn't going to wake up again, at least not in this world.

8

The people of Summerland had never realized before how much suspicion they generated in the community. This mysterious death under irregular circumstances brought out these suspicions, and the disappearance of Fred's wife entailed a great deal of investigation and publicity. The RCMP had to be called in, but they could find no trace of her. Samara was impressed with how gently they questioned the children. But Gus and Gina knew nothing. "Mommy went to do some important business."

"Do you know what kind of business?"

"Important business."

"Do you know where she went to do this business?"

"Downtown."

"She went downtown?"

"Yes, downtown."

"Will she be back soon?"

"Samara will take care of us until she comes back."

Gina put her arm around Samara's neck and clung to her.

The people of Summerland decided that they should have a simple funeral at once, and if the wife were found, they could have a memorial service with her.

Soon everyone at Summerland knew the terms of Fred's spoken will: Samara was to care for his children. There was, of course, no other subject of conversation but that of Fred's death, his wife's disappearance, the oddity of giving a twenty-year-old student the custody of two children.

"How will you manage?" Yuri asked at breakfast one morning.

"My parents are going to hire a housekeeper for me. Someone to do the cooking, laundry, that sort of thing, and babysit when I can't be home. Ron and Marty will be there too, but they've got their hands full. I think the authorities will find their mother soon."

"I don't think so," Raisa said.

"No? Why?"

"I think she does not wish to be found."

"You could be right. Well, all I can do is give it my best. If it doesn't work out, we'll come back to Boston at Christmas, and I'll go back to Tufts."

Several mornings later, Yuri sighed, hemmed, and at last stuttered out, "Raisa and I, we have a proposal."

"Yes?"

"We are wishing to apply for the position of your housekeeper. We will both do the job, but we will be paid as one."

"Boy, I'm overwhelmed. That would be wonderful. But would you want to move to St. Paul?"

"We have felt at peace here. We have bathed in the light, isn't that so, Raisa?"

Raisa smiled shyly, nodded, and lowered her eyes.

"We have said to each other often that someday we would like to have the care of little ones, especially little ones who have been hurt. We know too well what little ones can suffer."

"This would seem to solve my problem. I'll have to talk it over with my parents. And the kids. And Ron and Marty too. But it seems like a gift from heaven."

"To us, too, this seems like a gift from heaven."

For the remainder of the meal, Yuri described their accomplishments. Raisa, after her initial shyness, joined in too. Yuri, she said, could teach the children to play the violin.

"I didn't know you played the violin."

"Oh well, just a little bit."

"No, no, he is very good."

Raisa could cook, Yuri was handy with tools, Raisa knew about growing flowers. They would each begin at the university, taking only a few courses, and arranging their schedule so that there would always be someone home.

Samara was quite touched by the evidence that they had discussed the proposal thoroughly and in great detail. Her only qualm was one she wasn't sure she should confide to anyone. She finally decided this was too important a venture not to consult with her parents on everything. So she told them Raisa's secret, the scars. She repeated her suspicions of the relationship between the two, of the paucity of history, their secretiveness. Would someone who had been abused as a child then abuse the children in her care? It seemed to happen so often that those who were on trial for crimes against children had been abused when they were young. What did they know about these two, really?

It was Carol's suggestion that they invite Raisa and Yuri to their cabin for a discussion. Surely, she said, they would expect the Bellmonts to investigate the matter more fully.

Yuri put them at their ease. "Raisa and I think it's very important that you know our complete history. We both have suffered the consequences of a careless approach. We know you to be honorable, wise people. So we know you will not violate the trust invested in you. You will want to choose well."

Samara, with the help of her parents, had prepared some questions.

"Raisa, have you had any experience caring for children?"

But Raisa had steeled herself to her ordeal. Ignoring the question, she began:

"Yuri says I should tell you my whole story and withhold nothing. I was born in England of Russian émigrés. When I was five, my father died. Of a heart attack. My mother was not a prudent woman. She desired fine clothes, important friends. To obtain these, she became a spy. But she was not a very clever spy. When I was seven, she was arrested and imprisoned. I was sent to a foster home. There . . . "

She stopped. Yuri put his hand on her arm. He said, "I will tell this part. There she was molested sexually, and as her punishment for very slight offenses — missing some peel when peeling potatoes — she received the cigarette burns. You have seen the scars. Fortunately, after a period of time — two years, Raisa? Yes — this cruelty was discovered and she was sent to the group home where we met. The cook in our home was Canadian. Canada is the best country, she told us. Free and kind. So we applied to come here. Last September we were accepted."

"And now you want to emigrate to the United States? I don't think that is possible," Conway said.

"No, no. Not emigrate. We wish to go with Samara. We will return here."

"Perhaps they can come as my friends, as visitors."

"I think we can work something out. I'll get my lawyer on it right away. I'll call him first thing in the morning," Conway said. By this, Samara gathered that he was convinced.

Samara consulted with Ron and Marty.

"You might be a little crowded until Christmas. But then the couple in the other apartment are leaving — if he graduates, we can keep our fingers crossed — and they can have that apartment," Ron said.

Penny, discussing the plans with Carol, said, "Doesn't it reminds you of our early days together?"

"It does. I was saying that to Conway last night. The

difference — and I hope it doesn't mean trouble — is that they are going to have to live closer together."

"It's a lot of responsibility for a twenty-year-old."

"That's what's worrying me. It's really too much, way too much. Two months ago we were despairing that she didn't seem to have any goals, no sense of duty. It might be better if Gina and Gus stayed with us. At least for this year, until she got on her feet, got used to her duties with Marty. But she won't hear of it. She gave her word to Fred, she says, and she'll keep her word. Of course that pleases us — but it worries us too."

"Couldn't she postpone the St. Paul thing and stay with you this year?"

"We've discussed that possibility too. But she's so at sea at Tufts. And she's so excited about being a member of Marty's team. Whether or not she'll ever become a mathematician, or a physicist, she'll be in an environment of intellectual excitement, commitment. She's afraid to lose this opportunity."

"Anyway, she'll do fine."

The children were curiously grief-free. It seemed to Samara, and to everyone, that they should be a little more upset. They were stoic, matter-of-fact. They were so happy over ordinary things. To have clean clothes, clean sheets, regular baths, delighted both of them. They loved having Samara read them a bedtime story. Gus called out from bed, "Samara, bring me some juice." But he only sipped at it; clearly it was the power to make the demand that pleased him. Gina hollered, "Samara, we need you." And when she arrived, they giggled and made up an excuse. "You didn't kiss Puffy goodnight."

"We haven't been for our yearly walk," Samara said one evening.

"I thought you'd forgotten. You've been so busy. We've all been busy," Carol said, obviously pleased.

"We'll get Raisa to babysit tomorrow, if it's nice," Samara said. "We might not get another chance."

Out past the Richards' cottage, a rough path led along the top of a cliff. The tract of land had been bought, so it was rumored, by the Mafia as an investment, but nothing had ever been done with it.

"Don't forget your flute," Carol had said.

"I haven't played it for so long I probably can't get a note out of it."

As they walked along, Samara said "Everyone seems to be amazed that you and Dad have consented to my going. And with the kids."

"What are the alternatives? Make you stay with us? That doesn't seem fair. Make the kids stay with us? Have a seventy-eight year old man as a father? Their life would be as cheerless as it was with Fred. Of course I'm worried. Last night I had a terrible nightmare — you were kidnapped. It was so awful I woke up before I found out how it ended. I tried to will myself into dreaming again — so I could will a happy ending. I might have succeeded if I hadn't had to get up to pee."

When they reached the top of the cliff, Carol said, "I think I'm going to have to stay here. I could get down all right, but I'm afraid you'd need a crane to get me back up."

"You did O.K. last year."

"My knees were better last year. We can still do our thing — right here."

"Someone might see us."

"If they did they'd be so far away they wouldn't be able to tell what it was we were doing."

Samara got out her flute and began to play a strange improvised tune. Carol did a dancing, fluid version of tai chi, with the deep knee bending left out.

"It's rather nice doing it up here. It's so free and open."

Samara nodded her head but continued to play.

Sophie and Stevie proposed a sleepover at Sophie's two days before the end of Summerland. Samara said, "No, the kids would be bothered I think. You come here. We'll have the sleepover in the living room."

Gina assumed that she would be part of the sleepover. Samara heard her explaining to Gus, "It's only for girls. So don't feel bad. You can have a sleepover too. You can invite Ron. And Yuri too. I don't think you invite grownups. But you have to have beer. You know, like on television. I think boys go fishing on their sleepovers. I'll ask Ron what to do so you won't be embarrassed. Carol made popsicles for Samara. So Conway will make something for you. No, Conway doesn't cook. Can you remember? Do the boys eat popsicles with their beer?"

"They have things in dishes. They put their fingers in."

It began to get cold the night before the sleepover. Samara got up to make sure the children were covered. She got extra quilts out of the closet to put over them. Both of them slept on their backs with their hands up on the pillow. They looked so vulnerable in sleep; she was overwhelmed by the realization that she had to protect them.

In the morning the wind was blowing. Samara found sweaters and hats for her two charges, and they huddled together on the way to breakfast. Philip was up early to start the stove in order to take the chill out of the barn. The wind died down in the afternoon but picked up in the evening. Samara made a fire in the wood stove. Somehow, popsicles didn't have much appeal.

After the evening activities in the barn, Sophie, Stevie, Gina and Samara gathered in the living room. Conway had offered to put Gus to bed, read to him, and keep him company. The three women sat on mattresses on the floor in front of the stove; they leaned up against the couch. Gina snuggled in between Samara's legs and listened to the talk. By nine she was sound asleep. They could hear the wind blowing branches up against the house, and then heard a thud.

"Dad's bicycle blew over, I bet," said Samara.

"Summers are always weird, but this is the weirdest, don't you think?"

"Yes," Stevie said. "I feel as if I just looked on, like a spectator at a football game."

Sophie said, "Me, too. It was 'the year of Samara,' my mother said."

"That's a bit of an exaggeration," Samara said. "But I have felt like something has taken charge of me. That's kind of pretentious. But that's the way it feels."

"As if something said, I don't like the way Samara is going. I'll make her much more complex." Stevie laughed.

"Here you are, you're only twenty, and you've got two kids. It's unbelievable," Sophie said.

"And don't forget the others. I mean she's sort of second in charge of Marty. And Yuri and Raisa are just like children. They wander around like orphans or waifs."

"They'll look after me too, you know. My parents are counting on Marty to shape me up. And Yuri and Raisa will do a good job with the household affairs."

"And Ron? What part of Samara is he going to be in charge of?" Sophie said.

"We have a very platonic relationship. He's my buddy, that's all."

Samara's arms were getting tired, holding Gina. She shifted the little girl, put her flat on the mattress, and covered her up. She said, "That fire is making me sleepy. I'd better make sure Gus is O.K. before I doze off."

"Boy, we've become old fogies awfully fast. It's only ten and we're all sleepy."

"It's not carbon monoxide?"

"No, the stove is fine. The chimney too. The warmth and the wind outside makes it so cozy. But I'll let the fire die down."

It wasn't long before Stevie and Sophie were asleep. Samara closed up the stove, got back onto the mattress and snuggled down between Stevie and Gina.

Five minutes before, she had been so sleepy she could hardly keep her eyes open; now, suddenly, she was wide awake, her heart racing, her ears ringing, panic-stricken.

I can't bring up two children. I don't know anything about bringing them up. A new university. Being Marty's assistant. And what if Yuri and Raisa turn out to be mentally disturbed? You can be nice but still not be much use. Like Aunt Nita. I've never been to St. Paul. What do women wear there? What do children wear? What if the police find their mother and she's done something terrible? I don't think I can do this. I wasn't fair to Roger. Handled that badly. I know Stevie is hurt that I've ignored her this summer. What if I turn out to be like Fred? I could. His condition was inherited. Or what if Gus turns out to be like him? Why did their mother abandon them? Maybe they've inherited some mental illness from her. Have to remember to ask Marty if there are kitchen utensils in the apartment. Goodness, maybe there's not even furniture. No, I think Ron said it was furnished. Maybe I can stop my mind racing. I'll do deep breathing. No, I'll do centering. But all summer I have had trouble with centering. My mind wanders all over the place. Don't even know where my centre is. My feet are freezing. My head feels like someone took a spoon and stirred it up. I've got too much to do to get ready. I wish someone would wake up so I could talk it over.

She could hear the wind howling, even drowning out the roar of the ocean. It sounds like the middle of winter. It's going to be freezing by morning. I hope Gus stays covered up.

What was it that Fred saw, anyway? A yellow spot. What could that be? God, imagine if one of the kids comes to me some day and says, I see a yellow spot.

What a funny thing. My mother was an only child and wound up with all these people. And I'm an only child and I wind up with this whole crew.

Winterland

9

By September eighth the Bellmonts had still not heard
from Fred's wife, so on that day the five, Samara, Gus,
Gina, Yuri and Raisa, boarded the plane for Minneapolis.
Gina and Gus had the window seats and called out to each
other over the seat back, "Look at that" until they ran into
clouds.

Waiting to disembark, Samara began to help Gina put
on her jacket, while Yuri got down the carry-on luggage.
Gina's hand got caught in her sleeve. "You're hurting me,"
she cried out. A surge of anxiety hit Samara so hard it
buckled her knees. These four are all at my mercy. "Don't
get excited now. That can't hurt," she said, and fumbled
with the sleeve. Gina's hand slipped out, Yuri handed her
the gym bag containing her doll and its clothes, and they
all moved forward. Samara had Gina by the hand, Yuri had
Gus, and Raisa clutched Yuri's sleeve. My God, but we're
a strange-looking crew, Samara thought. They continued to
hunch together on the escalator. Samara's eyes were on the
stairs to make sure Gina's feet were securely set; halfway
down she raised her head and saw a beaming Ron waving
both arms. Samara had no free hand to wave back, so she
waggled her head and smiled.

At the bottom of the escalator, Ron picked up Gina and hugged her, leaned over and kissed Samara on the cheek. "Carry me, carry me," Gus was shouting, so Ron picked him up too and led the other three towards the luggage carousel. "Marty hated not to come to greet you," he said, "but she thought it made more sense for me to come alone so I could carry luggage, a beast of burden. She didn't say anything at all about carrying people."

"Billy's in here," Gina said, waving her bag.

"Who's Billy? Your cat?"

Gina and Gus laughed. "A cat would smother," Gus said.

"So why isn't Billy smothering?"

"He's her doll! Her old dead doll," Gus shouted.

"He's not dead!"

"What is he then, stupid?"

Gina looked at Samara, troubled. "What? He's not dead. What?"

Another surge of anxiety: I can't do this; it was crazy to think I could. "He's make believe. Not dead. Just make believe," Samara said.

When Ron set them down, Gina began to open her bag to show Ron. "Wait," Samara said. "Wait until we're in the van or else he might get lost." Gina looked around in alarm and yanked the zipper closed.

"Marty's so excited about your coming. She's had cleaning people there for three days — every inch of it has been scrubbed. And we've been planting flowers outside — kind of late I'd say to be planting flowers, but these are fall flowers. And bulbs, for next spring. Narcissus and tulips."

"I didn't know you had a yard," Samara said.

"We don't. A little patch in front and a little patch out back, but no one goes out there. Marty thought we could put a swing set for the kids there. You can decide."

They rode along in silence, Samara full of relief that the journey had been accomplished. Finally, Ron said, "Here's our street."

Samara was surprised that the neighbourhood was so

run down. Old car seats and sagging couches sat out on front porches. Cardboard boxes and strollers cluttered the small front yards, and instead of curtains some windows had sheets or flags stretched across them. In fact Samara knew Marty's house before Ron turned in because it looked so spruce. Ron must have been aware of the street's appearance. "This isn't as bad a neighbourhood as it looks. The university is assembling properties here, so a lot of the houses are rented by students. And most of the rest are inhabited by ancient widows. There are a lot of kids but not too many Gus and Gina's age. But we've been noticing that there are some."

Gina and Gus pushed their way out of the van and scooted up the stairs to the front porch. "We're here! We're here!" Gus shouted. "Open the door. We're here."

"Shh," Gina whispered. "She can't, remember?"

But the door opened with a seeing eye device, and as they stood there, the sliding door disappeared into its slot. Marty was sitting in the front hall.

"We're here," Gus said again, and the brother and sister clustered around Marty.

"See the new clothes Billy has," Gina was saying, yanking at the zipper. But it had got caught in the material of the bag and wouldn't open. She pulled and struggled, getting more upset until Samara appeared, carrying suitcases. "It won't open. It's stuck. Fix it, fix it!" Gina began to blubber.

"Now, now, this is very minor." Samara smiled at Marty. "I haven't even had a chance to say hello to Marty."

"Fix it, fix it!" Gina shrieked.

Samara sat down on the floor and took the gym bag in her lap. "See, the cloth is stuck in the zipper. That's nothing." She tugged at the material until it came loose and unzipped the bag. "Here." Gina threw her arms around Samara and began to sob. "Now, now. What's the matter. It's fixed. See, it's all fixed."

Gus was snuggling up against Samara, pulling at her blouse.

119

"Maybe they are afraid of me," Marty said. "Sometimes children are afraid of me."

"Of course not. They know you. I think there's just too much excitement, too much change."

Samara opened her arm to include Gus. Silent tears were flowing down his cheeks, as Gina's sobs began to subside.

"Don't you want to see where we're going to sleep? Our new home?" Samara said. Ron, Yuri and Raisa were making trips up and down the stairs. "Let's go upstairs and see." Marty spoke and Samara translated, "And then we'll come downstairs and have lemonade and cookies with Marty and Ron. Won't that be nice?"

One bedroom contained twin beds. In that room Yuri had put his and Raisa's suitcases. The other bedroom contained a double bed and a cot. Into that room Ron had put Samara's trunk, arrived two days before, and now he was setting Gina's suitcase there.

"This is where we'll sleep," Samara said. "You two will sleep in the big bed and I'll sleep in this bed. Let's hang some of our clothes in the closet."

She opened Gina's suitcase and took out a dress. "See, it didn't even get wrinkled. What a big closet. We'll be able to fit everything in here."

Gina was pulling out her underwear. "Where does this go?"

"What drawer do you want? Should I have the top one? And you have the middle one, and Gus can have the bottom one."

Samara opened Gus's suitcase. After they'd hung up a few things and put a few things in the drawers, Samara said, "Want to see the kitchen?"

They took a tour of the apartment. Gus discovered that there was pop and orange juice in the refrigerator.

"I have to pee," he said, so they went to find the bathroom.

Raisa was in the children's bedroom putting clothes away. "Aren't you coming down for lemonade?" Samara asked.

"No, I'll put these away. I can do ours tonight when the children are asleep. They will sleep better if the room looks untroubled."

"It's lovely of you to think of that."

But when bedtime came, they would not sleep. There was a funny shadow on the wall, they were thirsty, they had something to tell Ron, Gina wouldn't stop talking, Gus was taking up too much of the bed. Finally Samara, totally weary, decided to go to bed herself to settle the children down. She was asleep as soon as her head hit the pillow, and when she awoke in the night, cramped and sore, she discovered both children in bed with her. She crawled out of the cot and climbed into the double bed.

An odd tingling was invading her brain. It began in back of her eyes and spread to her ears, and gradually to the top of her head. The tingling became loud and insistent. She began to chew over the perplexities of the last month. Why had her parents allowed her, even encouraged her, to embark on this venture? The tingling persisted. I'm overtired I suppose. I'm too young for a stroke. Or a brain hemorrhage.

What would happen if the mother came back? Samara would just get attached to the kids and they would leave. Tomorrow her car would be delivered. Then she could go buy groceries. Raisa and Yuri would help with that. She'd continue Yuri's driving lessons. This new car had improved sensors, her father said, so Yuri could learn to park immediately.

Samara found it close to impossible to organize the daily routine of the household. She and Raisa would make out a schedule that seemed reasonable, but immediately something would come along to disrupt it. They had only been there two weeks when Gina came down with a virus and had to be home for three days.

A week later, on a Tuesday night, both Gus and Raisa

became sick too. Wednesday was the household's difficult day: Yuri's computer course ran all afternoon, Samara had a biology lab. Ron couldn't help out because he was terrified he would catch something and pass it on to Marty.

Samara was so tired from having been up all night with Gus that she made several awkward mistakes in the lab. When she arrived home, she came in on the middle of a quarrel between Yuri and Raisa. Raisa said she'd been too sick to take care of Gus, but she'd had to — she thought Yuri should have been willing to cut his class. Yuri argued that he couldn't do well in the course if he skipped a whole week of work. His plan had been to do so well in the course that he would be accepted into the regular program. Samara started supper but she let the potatoes boil dry, filling the apartment with smoke, setting off the smoke alarm.

Raisa's face was ghostly white. Both Yuri and Samara got frightened and wanted to take her to the emergency ward. Ron, seeing the state of affairs when he came up to check on the alarm, offered to go out and get hamburgers. Samara was almost too exhausted and discouraged to eat. In the morning, Raisa felt better and looked better too. Gus was entirely recovered.

One afternoon Samara walked home from class to find the house empty although both Marty's van and the new Volvo were in the driveway. Searching from room to room, she poked her head into the kitchen and could smell stew simmering on the stove. It's odd that they left the stove on while they went out. But maybe they're not going to be gone for long. Maybe they just all went for a walk around the block.

She could hear a tapping sound out back. That sounds like a woodpecker, she thought, and sat down on the couch to read the afternoon paper. The tapping continued, and at last bathroom window, she saw Gus and Gina dancing around the base of the lone tree, a catalpa. Raisa was looking up into the branches, clutching her hands to her face. Up in the tree, Yuri was pounding nails into boards. Ron was standing ready to hand him up another board. Samara raced downstairs and around the back.

The children began to shout, "It's a tree house. Our own house. Just ours. No one else's."

Marty was sitting on the back stoop.

"I gather this has your approval." Samara laughed, a little nervously.

"At first I thought they'd fall out of it. But Ron and Yuri persuaded us — Raisa and me."

Samara felt annoyance rising up in her. These were her children. Why hadn't she been consulted? Now it was too late. She'd be an ogre if she put her foot down. Her expression must have given her away, because Raisa hurried up to her. "Let me tell you," she said and took Samara by the hand, leading her down the driveway.

Out of earshot, Raisa said, "This is a bit dangerous. But not a lot. And we think it will keep them out of the street. This afternoon was a terrible time. Gina began to see her father. And she ran away. We were so frightened. But we found her just by the corner. And when Marty and Ron came home, we tried to think of a way to calm her. Yuri thought of this. It will be very safe. And in the book you bought, the one on how to bring up children, it says you should provide children with something just a little exciting."

Samara felt guilty for her annoyance. "What a terrific idea. They need something special. Fun. She saw her father?"

"She screeched 'he's in there' and pointed to the closet — the door was open. It was just the way your coat looked, I think — your black winter coat."

They moved again into the backyard. Marty was laughing — a mournful intake of breath. Yuri had caught his pants on a limb and was unable to get it unfastened. Ron was lifting Gus up onto the platform to help Yuri, and Gina was demanding to be allowed up too.

"The poor catalpa tree," Samara said to Marty. "It won't know what hit it."

"Yes," Marty said. "To be so lonely and now to be the center of attention."

"It's probably happy now," Raisa said.

Yuri finished making the basic platform. Gina was allowed to get up onto it, and Raisa announced that supper was ready.

"We'll work on it tomorrow after school," Yuri consoled the children. "It will take many days to make it perfect. But tomorrow you will be able to be up here to help me."

That night Samara dreamed of the catalpa tree, a dream so vivid that it woke her. She and an old man in a wool suit were dancing on the platform, dancing so vigourously that one of her shoes flew off and fell to the ground. The man was happy and at the end of the dance, he looked at her with a beaming, loving smile and said, This is the high point of my life.

Awake, she kept dreaming the dream. The dance continued; the platform enlarged until it held many couples, all poor, rough-looking. In fact minute by minute they became more menacing until Samara realized there were no women there; the couples were men. The men had dirty shirts and pants, greasy hair, sneers, mean eyes.

It was generous of Marty to let Yuri build a tree house in the only tree they had. All those nails and pounding couldn't be doing the tree any good, Samara thought. When she came home from class the next day, the children each had a small hammer and were helping Yuri put up walls. Raisa was sitting on the back stairs sewing striped green curtains.

"I'm glad you are home. They have almost run out of wood, and Yuri has no more money."

"Did he buy the wood?"

"Yes, of course."

"I didn't even think of where the wood came from. He shouldn't spend his money on the children."

"He likes to spend his money that way. But we have had expenses, as you know."

"What a dear he is."

"Yes."

When Gina spotted Samara, she called out, "There's no more wood. What will we do? Gus wants to get a job. Yuri says we're too young. But I don't know."

"Come and see," Gus began.

"Will it hold all four of us, Yuri?"

"Most certainly. You have no faith in my ability as a carpenter? For shame. This ladder is just temporary so be careful. We have to figure out a way to build a ladder that can be pulled up after them. Ron says he will put his mind to this technical problem."

"This is magical. It's so snug. And yet so exhilarating."

"That's a good word. Exhilarating."

"So, Gus, you need money? I tell you what. If you and Gina make my bed every morning for a week, I'll pay you enough to buy the wood. Is that fair?" Samara said.

Gus beamed. "We'll do it way way longer."

"A week is good enough."

"Now we have to wait until Ron and Marty come home with the van so we can get the wood," Yuri said.

Samara asked if the house was going to have a roof.

"Samara! What kind of a house doesn't have a roof? Yes. Ron suggested a canvas roof arranged like a wing of a bird. He has a picture of it in his mind."

Saturday morning they all worked on the house, now called "Wingspread." But they had to stop at lunchtime because Marty's department was having an open house, and they all were going. Gus whined a bit.

"Why do Yuri and I have to go? We can stay here and work on the house."

"Me too," Gina said.

"Shh," Raisa said. "Do you want to hurt Marty's feelings? She thinks we really want to go."

At the open house, Samara said to Raisa, "Marty's like a queen on her throne." Yuri carried Gus everywhere, explaining each experiment, each exhibit, until Gus began to squirm and beg to get down. But Yuri was obviously so disappointed not to be able to finish the tour that Raisa offered to take the children to the cafeteria where refreshments were being served. He and Samara continued to wander, stopping for the demonstrations, asking questions.

"Did you realize how important she is?" Yuri asked.

"No, I can't say as I did. I knew she was important, but not this much."

"I feel guilty that she spends so much time on us."

"I think we make her happy though. Like a family."

"Perhaps."

At four Ron came to find them. "Marty's exhausted. I'm going to take her home."

"Perhaps Raisa and the children can go with you. I'll get them. Samara and I are nearly finished. We'll be along in a half hour or so."

When they had completed the tour, Yuri said, "Let's go back to the Circulator for a few minutes. I think I'll understand it better now."

It had been decided that to ease Samara into being an aide to Marty this first term, she would assist at Marty's office hours. The language would not be quite so technical as it would be even in Marty's undergraduate course. And this was the activity Ron liked least. Samara could tell he liked his public performance in Marty's classes, but sitting "listening to all the wimps and whiners" had by now become tedious, he said. For Samara the sessions were like private tutoring, something she needed because Marty's class was the first real challenge she'd ever had.

She took her cue from Ron and adopted his technique

in her office sessions. Instead of literally translating
Marty's words to the class, he conducted a kind of
dialogue with her. The result of this was that instead of the
class becoming boring — not only one droning lecture but
two — the class was exotic yet human. Two minds were
playing off each other. Ron could ask the questions that
made things plainer. And underlying the dialogue about
matroid theory, a human drama was going on, which,
Samara soon discovered, everyone in the class was aware of.

One of the difficulties Samara had faced in registering Gina
and Gus for school was that neither of them knew their
birthday. But that was only the first of many mysteries.
Had they had any vaccinations? Fred had suggested they
had both been to school, but neither of them seemed to
remember. What grade were they to be put in? Gina could
read and write very well, but she seemed to know nothing
about numbers. Raisa discovered in them a surprising
pocket of learning: each knew a great deal about
astronomy. When the time changed back to standard at the
end of October, the whole household went outside after
supper and the children pointed out constellations and
stars. They both remembered and described vividly the
time their mother and father had awakened them in the
middle of the night and had driven out of the city so that
they could see the Comet Boren, nicknamed "The
Unexpected." In October, too, a private detective hired by
Conway had discovered their births recorded in Indiana
and sent birth certificates. Titre tests determined that the
children were not immunized against anything.
    On the morning of November first, Yuri asked Samara
if she were going to be home that evening. "It's Raisa's
birthday and I would like to take her to dinner. And I
noticed that there is an interesting play in Minneapolis."
    "Sure. I'll be able to come home early. Maybe you'd like
to go for a drive — explore a bit — before dinner."

During a break between classes, Samara bought a gift from herself and one each from Gina and Gus. She also bought a cake mix and some candles, and before supper she and the children made the cake.

"When they come home, I'll wake you up and we'll have a party. I bet you've never been to a birthday party at midnight!"

In November, too, the detective found Fred's wife, living with a man in a town forty miles from Cleveland. The man had been a colleague in the real estate firm Fred's wife worked for. Now they had started their own agency. The detective had mystifying news. The children, Fred's wife said, were not hers. They were the progeny of Fred's first wife. She had been killed in a car accident; suicide had been suspected. The second wife seemed to be relieved that her involvement in "that weird set-up" was over, but she also expressed remorse and guilt. She told the detective that she had wondered why they weren't back on York Street. She had "cruised around there quite a few times." She thought they'd decided to stay with Fred's father. She assured the detective that she had intended to inquire after a while.

Why hadn't Fred told anyone — Samara or his father — this story? Was it true that Gus and Gina were the children of a first wife? Why was there no hint of it from the children?

It was Saturday morning. Samara had on Friday handed in the research essay that had been troubling her for two weeks. She was standing at the kitchen sink washing the dishes. If she stood on her tiptoes and leaned over the sink, she could look down into the tree house where Gina, Gus, and Ron were constructing a built-in picnic table. Yuri and Raisa were grocery shopping; Marty, Samara was sure, was sitting on the back porch watching the tree people. While she was doing the dishes, Samara was also

making molasses cookies. She was taking out the third
batch when she heard a noise on the stairs — Yuri and
Raisa back from shopping. They all felt like celebrating.
Unusually warm weather had been forecast; already Samara
could see that Ron had taken off his jacket and rolled up
his sleeves.

"We're back," Raisa called when she opened the door to
the apartment. As she was making her way across the
living room, the phone rang and Samara answered it. Yuri,
coming through the living room into the kitchen, said, "I
think it must be Fred's wife." Raisa went to the door and
looked on, her forehead puckered in worry.

"They seem to be doing O.K. Gus has bad dreams every
once in a while. They talk about you. But I think Fred
must have convinced them that you were gone for good."

Samara looked up and saw Raisa's worried expression.
She motioned with her finger to the living room and made
the gesture of holding an imaginary phone to her other ear.
Raisa looked perplexed. Samara covered the phone with
her hand and half-whispered, half-mouthed, "Listen in,"
again pointing to the living room and holding an imaginary
phone. Raisa was not certain whether she meant "Go away
and don't eavesdrop" or "Pick up the other phone," but as
her heart so thoroughly wanted her to listen in, she took
the second meaning. She heard Samara say, "What will we
do? How can we clear this mess up?"

And she heard Fred's wife say, "I don't know how you
feel. They must be a bother. Going to school and looking
after two kids must be a pain. Wouldn't you rather I come
get them? Or you could send them on a plane."

"We're pretty well set here. There's lots of people to
look after the kids. And they aren't much bother. So if it's
O.K. with you, we'd just as soon have them stay here. At
least for the time being."

Fred's wife sounded relieved. "Sure, it's O.K. with me. I
know they're being looked after well. I'm kind of surprised
you're not all back in Massachusetts with your parents,

but I think you've got good judgment about the babysitters."

"We've got the best. I don't know if you met Raisa and Yuri. But they're here. And Ron helps out too — remember him? — he was the one who looked after the lady in the wheelchair? She's the one whose house we're staying in. The kids seem pretty content. They seem to like their school. And there's one other thing — I did promise Fred I'd look after them. They are my own flesh and blood. To tell you the truth, to put it bluntly, we love them dearly and would miss them awfully. I mean all of us love them."

"The funny thing is that I love them dearly too. And I miss them. But I'm burned out. That's what happened to their mother — burned out. Fred was a lovely man. But living with him day in and day out was impossible. Put you right on the edge, believe me."

"I understand. I sure do. So it's settled then. They'll stay here?"

"That's the best thing, don't you think?"

"I do. One more problem. Shall I tell them you called?"

Raisa wasn't interested in hearing anymore. She put the phone down, tiptoed into her bedroom, closed the door, lay down on the bed, and sobbed.

A minute later, Yuri was knocking on the door. "Raisa, can we come in? What's the matter? Why are you crying?"

"Come in," she said.

Yuri and Samara, standing in the door, saw her sobbing yet with a sickly smile on her face. "I'm so happy — I feel I could fly."

On a Thursday night in the middle of November Samara realized she would have to stay up late to finish a paper. Until they could occupy the two apartments in Marty's house, they had decided to put the computer in Raisa's and Yuri's room.

"It would be no trouble to move it into the living room," Yuri said. "But I think a better solution would be that I sleep on the hide-a-bed and Raisa sleep with the children. That way, if they wake up, Raisa can tend to them."

"I hate to disrupt your sleep. Raisa's especially."

"You must not consider that," Raisa said. "I will sleep well hearing the children breathing."

The children at first were excited about the change, but as bedtime approached they became apprehensive. "What if," "What if" began each sentence.

"Raisa takes care of you during the day. Why do you think she can't take care of you at night?"

As the hours wore on, Samara got more and more panicky that she wasn't going to finish. She was too tense to be sleepy, but too exhausted to be wide awake. At three-thirty she went into the kitchen to make herself another cup of strong coffee. Turning toward the sink, she knocked the mug off the counter onto the floor, shattering it and spilling the dregs of coffee. At that moment, Gus screamed. Damn, I woke him up, Samara thought. He screamed again, and by the time she had got to his room, bedlam had set in with Gina crying, Raisa shouting for Samara and Yuri struggling to come up out of his sleep.

"Gus, Gus. It's O.K. I just dropped a mug in the kitchen. That was the noise. Just a cup breaking."

Raisa was trying to hold him in her arms, saying, "There, there."

Gus struggled to get free of her and continued to scream.

"Stop it, Gus. Stop that noise! There's nothing wrong."

"Gina, Gina," he began to call.

"She's here. Right here."

"Get away!" he hollered. "Gina." He thrashed and batted at their arms. He screamed again, a terrified high-pitched noise that seemed louder than a small boy could make.

"Stop it," Samara shouted back. But the noise continued.

She raised her hand and hit the side of his face. The screaming stopped, became a whimper, "Gina, Gina."

"Oh my God. I hit him. Raisa. I slapped his face. My God, my God." Samara buried her face in Raisa's shoulder.

Yuri took charge. "Gina. Talk to your brother. Hold him. There now, give him a hug. Tell him you're Gina. Speak to him."

"Here I am. Here is Gina. Everything is fine. Don't be afraid."

She babbled on, holding his hand, kissing his hair.

They all were startled to hear Ron's voice at the bedroom door. "What's wrong? Can I do something?"

"Put the light on," Yuri said.

Ron stood in the doorway, his bare legs and feet sticking out of a rain poncho. He was wringing his fingers and cracking his knuckles. "Who's hurt?"

Raisa lifted her head. "Gus had a nightmare, I guess. Samara dropped a cup on the floor. It scared him maybe."

Ron came into the room and knelt down beside the bed. "Hey little guy. You have a bad dream?"

Yuri stood beside him, and on the other side of the bed, Raisa sat with one arm around Samara, the other hand patting Gus's back.

Raisa said to Gus, "Now you can sleep right in between Gina and me. Yuri will sleep in Samara's bed. And we'll all be safe and cozy."

When they were tucked in, Samara put out the light and Ron closed the door. Samara went into the kitchen and began picking up shards of mug. Ron took some paper towels and mopped up the coffee. They sat at the table.

"I slapped him."

"Gus? Was that what all the fuss was about?"

"No, he was screaming and he wouldn't stop. I slapped him. I can't believe I did such a terrible thing. The poor little kid scared out of his mind and I slapped his face. It's just too much — being a mother to all this and trying to go to school. I can't do it. My paper's due this morning. No extension he said."

"You're doing a great job. A wonderful job. Four waifs have a home because of you. So you made a mistake. So you're not perfect. Did you expect to go through life being perfect?"

"Two kids. I'm only twenty. What were my parents thinking of?"

"It seems overwhelming now at — what? — four in the morning. Everything is overwhelming then. That's why people are usually in bed at that time. But now, let's get the paper done. Have you got anything down?"

"Sure."

"How many pages?"

"Thirty."

"How long is it supposed to be?"

"He didn't say. Or did he? As long as it takes, I guess."

"Thirty pages seems like enough to me. Now you just write, 'That's all I have to say — goodbye.'"

"That's not funny. I haven't even half-finished."

"So you say 'This is the first chapter, the preliminaries, and I'll write the second chapter for the next paper.'"

"He wouldn't allow that."

"The alternative is not to hand in anything and flunk. Maybe he won't like this and give it a C. On the other hand, maybe he'll go for the idea. Let's finish it. Let me go down and get some clothes on and explain to Marty."

In a few minutes Ron was sitting at the computer; he

read the last few pages, made some suggestions. "Now you dictate two concluding paragraphs to me and I'll type."

It took a few more paragraphs than two, but by six the paper was finished.

"Let's get some breakfast. We'll bring back donuts for a treat for the rest. I'll put my shoes on and meet you at your car."

Samara scribbled a note for Raisa.

In the car, she said, "Can you leave Marty?"

"She's awake. And I've got the pager." He patted his belt. "She's all right."

They stopped in front of Frenchy's.

Samara said, "I'm not dressed well enough to go in there. I don't think I've even combed my hair."

"At six-thirty people won't be dressed in gowns. I've been wanting to try their breakfast. It's supposed to be great."

The waitress poured their coffee and set the carafe on the table. They ordered waffles and sausages.

"This is exciting. The second time we've been alone together," Ron said.

"The second time?"

"Don't you remember the first? When we went into town at Summerland?"

"I remember it of course. But this couldn't be only the second time. We must have been alone since then."

"When? You tell me."

"I don't know. I can't think of a specific time."

"Because there hasn't been one. Don't you feel free as a bird?"

"I guess I'm too tired to feel free."

"You feel better though? You've got the paper done."

"Yes, I feel better. But I still don't know how I can manage. Slapping him. Unbelievable. So evil."

Samara closed her eyes and shook her head.

"Not evil. Just human. I hurt Marty once."

"You did?"

"After one of her choking sessions. I was so scared. And then relieved. And an hour or so later I came in and found her trying to open one of her pill jars. With a childproof cover. What are you doing I said. It's not time for your pill. And then I knew — she was going to take them all. I took them and threw the jar across the room and grabbed her and shook her and shook her, and . . . . I stopped and everything went black — it was as if my soul was cringing down at the bottom of my brain and there was no way to get out — no way to contact the outside world. Finally — I don't know how long it was — I heard Marty sobbing — a long way off — and I knew I was sobbing too. Gradually I came to the surface — came out of the dark into the light of day. She was sobbing and couldn't tell me if I'd hurt her."

"You must have felt terrible."

"Worse than terrible. I'd wake up in the night thinking about it, and the only way I could stand it was to moan — make funny sounds. The thing is — you know you can only do something like that once. Like they say about a dog — he's allowed one bite — the second one, he's gone."

"I hope, I pray, I'd never do such an awful thing again."

"You know what? I think we should get out more often — do something fun away from them. Just relax. I know Yuri and Raisa wouldn't mind. For that matter, they should get out too."

"Would Marty feel bad do you think? Feel left out? If we went to the movies or something?"

"She wouldn't. She's always saying I should get out."

"But with me? Would that hurt her feelings?"

"Why you? She loves you. She thinks you're great."

"But would she think, if we went to the movies, that it was, I don't know, like a date. As if I was horning in. She's so fond of you."

"Oh that. The boy-girl thing. No, it's not like that

between Marty and me. Not at all. Christ, if it was like
that between us, it would be impossible. Or I'd have to get
castrated or something."

Samara wasn't convinced, but she dropped the subject.

It had been planned before they came to St. Paul that they
all would fly home for the Thanksgiving recess. But as the
time approached, Samara, Yuri and Raisa decided that it
would be too disruptive for the children, so Carol and
Conway agreed to come there for the holiday. They would
arrive the Saturday before and leave the Monday after
Thanksgiving.

Neither of them were prepared for the change they
found in Samara. Carol said to her, "We didn't like your
devil-may-care attitude and now we're fussing about your
super-responsibility. Just like a Bellmont — excessive — the
pendulum swinging from one side to the other."

"Your mother's right. Never a happy medium with us."

"Can you think of anything more we could do to help?"
Carol asked.

"You're doing everything humanly possible. When we
can have the two apartments it will be better. We're so
packed in. None of us ever gets a chance to be free of the
kids, even at night."

Raisa had the turkey in the oven by eight and by nine
Carol had arrived in a taxi to start making pies. Yuri and
Samara began to peel the vegetables and Gus and Gina had
the job of picking over the cranberries. For every
questionable berry, they had to run to one of the adults
for an opinion, yea or nay. Carol was using Marty's
kitchen for baking the pies; they would eat in Marty's
ample dining room; Ron and Marty were in charge of
decoration and table-setting. When the berries were all

inspected and washed, Raisa supervised the measuring of water and sugar — Gus the water and Gina the sugar.

In shifts, they went out for walks; at four o'clock, the ten of them sat down to dinner.

Marty said, as Ron translated, "Conway, would you honour us by saying grace?"

"Yes, thank you." He shut his eyes and for ten or fifteen seconds there was complete silence. Then he began, slowly, and there could be no doubt that he was speaking directly to God,

"Help us to be single of heart so that we may see Your face. Hold everyone gathered here in the palm of Your hand. Make us grateful."

There was silence for another ten seconds and then Gus said, "I saw a field with red flowers and it smelled just like sandwiches."

"Sandwiches?" Raisa asked.

"When we went on our picnic where we found the grapes."

11

The next four weeks were difficult for everyone. First Gina and then Gus got colds and had to stay home from school for two days. Gina was left with a cough which nothing seemed to help. Raisa and Samara took turns sleeping with her in Raisa's room because her coughing woke Gus. Yuri slept on the hide-a-bed for four nights and got a backache which made his right knee buckle at unpredictable times. Samara had papers and lab reports due, and, in the third week of December, final exams. Every few days she'd think, I will not be able to do this.

Yuri had a computer project due and an exam, and

although he never complained, his worry manifested itself in an uncontrollable shudder that would pass over him. Every time Gina had a violent coughing spell, Raisa would become so terrified she'd unconsciously hold her breath.

They also had to make plans for Christmas. It seemed sensible that Yuri and Raisa would move into their apartment while Samara and the children were in Boston. Yuri looked forward to this, to painting and wallpapering and shopping for second-hand furniture. To a certain extent Raisa did too. But she also knew she would miss Gina and Gus, especially Christmas day.

Samara could not spend energy looking any further than December nineteenth. Over and over she told herself, One day at a time. She had a stroke of luck: she brought a paper late to the professor's office and discovered that he hadn't picked up the essays yet. Samara could see the pile of papers on his floor through the slot in his door, and there was a sign: Due to illness Professor Blaney won't be in his office for regular office hours Wednesday and Thursday.

After Samara's last exam, late in the afternoon as she was waiting for the elevator, she remembered that it was nearly the shortest day of the year. She looked out a window of the eleventh floor across the Mississippi River to the lights of the city on the other side. A building, not one of the tallest but still tall enough to be called a skyscraper, had decorated its upper stories with Christmas lights. From her angle of vision Samara could see no design, but several of the red and blue lights seemed to be popping straight up, or exploding, or perhaps just blinking on and off. From that distance she couldn't tell whether the lights were supposed to be doing that or whether there was some malfunction, a short circuit, even an electrical fire. The elevator arrived, but she ignored it and continued to look out the window. After watching for five minutes, she was reassured by the regularity of the popping and she pushed the down button again. But all the way home she kept glancing to her left to see if she could see flames. At nine, right before she was going to crawl into bed, she put on the radio for the local news. There was no mention of disaster in downtown Minneapolis, so she slept the sleep of the just, of the hard-working, of the well-fed.

The next afternoon Samara went out to shop for her housemates' Christmas presents. "I'll be back in time to help get supper," she said to Raisa. "For the first time in quite a while."

"Take your time. Supper is easy tonight. We'll eat late — maybe six — that will give you plenty of time."

Raisa was easy to buy for — she had nothing and loved everything pretty — jewellery and a silk scarf for her. For Yuri, an electric saw — she'd heard him tell Ron how handy one would be. For Ron, an orange and brown sweater. Marty was the difficult one. Finally at four, Samara gave up and bought her a vase, but as handsome as it was, she thought it was a defeat. As she was coming out of the deli in St. Paul where she had bought eclairs for a special dessert, she met a student who was a regular at Marty's office hours. "I finished my last exam an hour ago. Now I'm celebrating. Come have a drink with me," he said.

"I've got time — just an hour or so. Sure."

They walked to one of the favourite university hangouts, Calvino's. The young man was handsome and charming, she thought, and sitting across from him, with a beer, a tingle of excitement passed over her. Several beers later, she said, "What's the time?"

"Nine-thirty."

"Damn. I was going to be home by six. I've got to go. See you after the break. Merry Christmas."

When she left the tavern, she felt very light-headed. I can't drive like this. I'll walk until I see a taxi. Or maybe a phone booth. As she walked she became more and more unsteady and confused. Waves of near-unconsciousness passed over her, and the fright from these began to sober her up. Yet, time seemed to stand still; she wasn't quite sure where she was, and she began to realize that she was walking alone after dark. Up ahead was a phone booth. Raisa answered, "Dear heavens. Thank you dear Lord. We thought you were kidnapped. Or murdered. Yuri is out looking for you, on foot. But where would he find you in this big city? Like looking for a needle in the straw. Yes, Yes, I'll go right down and tell Ron to get you."

Samara began to feel nauseated and then faint again. What a stupid thing I've done. Poor Raisa. Poor Yuri. Oh if we only all get back to our apartment safe and sound, I'll never do this again. She heard footsteps on the sidewalk and saw two men coming toward her. This is it. I'll never get back home. Never. What a dumb thing. She went back into the phone booth and closed the door. The two men walked on by. She was afraid she was going to vomit, dirtying the booth. Where's Ron? He probably can't find this place.

A young maple tree had been planted in a drain for the sidewalk. Samara determined to climb the tree. I can see Ron coming, she thought, but I'll be safer from rapists. Will those limbs hold me? She shinnied up the trunk. I'm ruining this coat. Once up in the branches, she realized she could be seen clearly and was not much if any safer. But she sat there precariously, uncomfortably, and wept.

A car was slowing down, a familiar sound, the roar of the van. She screamed, Ron! Ron. He put his head out the window and hollered, "I'll park over in that driveway. Stay there and I'll help you down."

He came running. "What in God's name are you doing up in a tree? Where have you been? Raisa is hysterical. I mean really hysterical." He positioned himself under the branch and Samara tried to let herself down.

"I'm afraid I'll vomit on you."

"Vomit? Are you sick?"

"Not exactly."

"You've been drinking. I can smell it. All of us in an

uproar and you out carousing. You promised Raisa to be home by six."

"I'm sorry. So sorry."

She let go the branches and slid down onto his shoulders. His hands steadied her until she was sitting astride his shoulders, holding onto his head, he grasping her left knee. Her right leg was caught up in her coat and was sticking out at a crazy hurting angle. Ron strode off toward the car. Samara couldn't say that her leg hurt or even ask to be put down. When they got to the van, he lowered her onto the roof and grabbed her as she slid off. He opened the door and sat her on the seat. They drove home in silence. At their house, Samara got out of the car and began to walk toward the door. Ron picked her up roughly and carried her upstairs. Raisa, Gina and Gus were standing at the door of the apartment. Ron brushed by them and lowered Samara onto the couch and walked back out without a word.

Raisa knelt down on the floor, buried her face in Samara's lap. Gus and Gina scrambled up onto the couch one on each side of Samara and took locks of her hair in their hands, holding her hair to their mouths. In a few moments Yuri came in. He'd gone out without a hat and he was holding his ears.

"Now, now," he said, pulling Raisa up. "It has all turned out well. So no need to fret."

She smiled a half-smile. "Now we need to eat supper. We aren't angels you know." And Raisa smiled more broadly at her own joke.

"You haven't eaten yet?" Samara said.

After supper Yuri went out to get the car, and he brought in the packages.

"I'll wrap them tomorrow," Samara said. "I'll have time before we have to leave for the plane."

In the morning, Samara waited for Ron and Marty to come to say goodbye but there was no call or visit. On the way down to the car, Samara knocked on the door. Marty opened the door with the electric eye.

"We've come to say goodbye and wish you a Merry Christmas."

"We'll miss you. But we'll take good care of Yuri and Raisa. Ron's parents have invited us all over for Christmas dinner. Here are our presents for you and the children."

"And here are ours for you. And for Ron."

"He's gone out just now."

"Wish him a Merry Christmas for me, for us. And say goodbye."

"Yes."

Samara could sense Marty's awkwardness. Had Ron told her about last night? Was he still angry? Of course. That was why he had gone out.

On the way to the airport she was silent. I make one little mistake and everyone acts as if I'd committed murder. Just one tiny error. It isn't fair. Here I am saddled with all these people — kids and cripples and losers and trying to go to school and run a house, and I take two hours out for a little fun and what happens? They act as if I was the wickedest woman in North America.

But of course the "they" was "he."

After she'd been home a day, she unburdened herself to her mother.

"His reaction was extreme. But he was disappointed. And maybe a little jealous."

"Why jealous? We're just friends. Buddies. We're not going together."

"Now you're being disingenuous. Surely you know that he cares for you as more than a buddy."

"Then why doesn't he say so? Why doesn't he ask me to go out? He never even asks me to go to the movies or anywhere alone."

"Because you both have obligations of course. Neither of you is free to have an ordinary boy-girl thing. He'd probably like to go out for a night on the town too. He thought you were both in it together — denying yourselves for duty."

"You're right. I guess I really knew that. And he has said a few things. Not much."

"Does Marty love him — as a man, I mean?"

"He says no, but I have a feeling she does. How could she help it?"

"Yes. I'd be willing to bet on it."

"What can she say? If she tells him, their relationship will become impossible. He'd either have to marry her or leave her. She's smart enough to know that."

"What about him?"

"I think he loves her like a child. Or a sister. I'm sure he doesn't have any sexual feeling for her at all."

"Poor Marty. It's all pretty complicated. I suspect she knows just how much more complicated it could get. And it may be dawning on him too. Hence the extreme reaction."

Later on, while they were beginning a game of *Pilgrimage*, Samara said, "A further complication, about Yuri and Raisa. Raisa to be exact. She has fallen in love with the kids. I looked back as we were leaving and tears were streaming down her face. And the night I — well, misbehaved — she apparently had been hysterical. Yuri likes us all well enough. He's really fond of us. But for him Raisa is the one."

"He's probably kind of glad to have her to himself for a few weeks."

"I think so. And I think he'll like having their own apartment."

Conway said, "I'm quite impressed with Gina and Gus. They seem so much better than they did. Your mother agrees. You've done a wonderful job."

"Thanks. Raisa deserves the credit. Yuri and Ron too."

"That may be. But we can read between the lines, you know. It's quite clear that you're the center. Needless to say, we're proud."

Basking in their approval, playing the familiar intense game, Samara could feel herself shedding fears, doubts, even guilt. She thought, I'll call them when we finish the game. It will only be nine there. I'll call both apartments. No, I'll wait and call Raisa in the morning so the kids can speak to her. But I'll call Ron and Marty tonight.

Conway said, "You're rusty. That was a dumb move."

"You didn't play fair. You got me thinking about St. Paul. You spoiled my concentration."

"It was your mother. She's deadly when it comes to psychological warfare."

"Whereas your father always wins on his brains alone."

The game, however, swung round, Conway found the treasure, but Samara was able to intercept him, and so it was she who wound up with the Holy Grail.

"I'm going to call Ron and Marty. O.K.?"

"Certainly. What about Raisa and Yuri?"

"I thought I'd call them in the morning. Then Gina and Gus could talk. Raisa would like that better."

"Do you want some advice?"

"Maybe." She smiled.

"Apologize."

"I was going to try to. It will be kind of awkward."

Ron couldn't keep the joy out of his voice. Samara was encouraged to plunge in. "Ron, I have something to say. I feel terrible about that evening. It was so thoughtless. And stupid. Your good opinion means a lot to me. Yours and Marty's."

"Don't mention it. I overreacted. Marty has been lambasting me ever since you left. I apologize. Now we're both off the hook."

"Great."

"You'll have to wait for your present. I was kind of sulking and put it back in my room."

Two days before Christmas, Gus stopped talking. In the bustle of the season Samara did not notice right away. He would not speak to Raisa on the phone. At suppertime she observed his worried look and waited for him to speak. Gina rattled away, but there was no talk of Christmas. Before bedtime Samara took Gus off to the den and sat him on her lap.

"Is something bothering you, honey?"

Silence. Samara hugged him to her and clasped his head to her chest, stroking his hair. Then she could hear little intakes of breath, feel his body trembling. Tears were creeping down his cheeks. "Are you homesick for St. Paul? For Raisa? We'll be going back in ten days, you know."

Silence except for the intakes of breath.

"Is anything hurting?"

Silence.

Samara began to rock herself and Gus back and forth. Finally, "Samara?"

"Yes."

"We don't know what's Christmas."

"You've had Christmas before? Your daddy and mommy celebrated Christmas, didn't they?"

"We don't know what's Christmas."

"It's like a birthday party. Like Thanksgiving. Only bigger. Our Christmas tree is part of the decoration for it. And Christmas morning we'll give each other presents. As if it were everyone's birthday the same day. And we'll have a nice, special dinner. We're celebrating. It's really very nice. A lot of fun. You and Gina will love it, I guarantee."

"Mommie didn't like it. It was very bad. No good."

"I guess some people, your mommie, think it makes people greedy. They just want presents. They don't think of other people, just themselves. But we won't be like that, will we? You'll think of me, and I'll think of Gina, and Gina will think of Grampie Bellmont. And Grampie will think of Carol. We'll make a big effort."

Silence.

"I tell you what. If you don't like Christmas — if you get scared or unhappy — we'll stop it right there. You just say stop and hold up your hand like this, and we'll stop Christmas. Right then and there. And have just a regular day. We'll put up a big sign that says Go away Christmas. What do you think of that?"

Silence. Then a trembling, but brave, "O.K."

That evening Conway went out and bought four children's books about Christmas. He had a hard time finding a book on Gus's age level that still was simple enough, still explained enough. Samara went up in the attic and got out her children's books. There was *Grandmother's Wonderful Chair with the story of the Christmas Cuckoo, and a beautifully illustrated Night Before Christmas.* The next morning, she read the six stories to the children. After that, all morning long, Gus sat on the couch and pored through the books, studying each page, his brow wrinkled, deep sighs coming from his skinny chest. Just before lunch Samara asked him if he'd
like her to read them again and he smiled and nodded yes.

One of the books Conway bought was the story of Jesus's birth with a picture of the cave, the manger and cows. As Samara was about to turn the page, he clapped his hand over it. "What's that?"

"That's a cave in the rocks. Like a hole in the rocks. And that's where the animals live."

"Like at Summerland."

"You mean the barn?"

"Down by the water."

"The grotto! Yes. Just like that, only bigger."

The adults took turns reading to Gus and in between he read to himself. Once he called out to Gina, "I'll read you the books." She came and sat on the couch with him while he went through all six of them. He would stop on nearly every page to give her his explanation. Samara stood outside the living room door and listened.

"This is an elf. They call him Tomten. He's a teeny little man. The cows are scared because it's dark. And cold. So he's talking to them nice. Elves are like Santa Claus. They're spirits. They can go up to heaven and come down anytime they want to. God and Jesus and Daddy are like that too." And later. "There's Santa Claus coming down through a hole in the roof. Don't be afraid of him. He doesn't really look like that at all. He's in the air. Grampie says if you don't want him to come near you, you just wave your arm like this and he'll blow away." And later, "I don't know why these spirits come around. Well, it's just to leave us presents. Daddy will probably leave us a present."

And later, "These men are leaving presents. It's a cup. I don't know what Daddy will leave us. It has to come through a hole in Grampie's roof. Probably he will leave a ball. Or maybe a cup. But if you don't want him to come you wave your arm like this."

Carol reported that evening that she had heard Gus say to Gina, "When you look in the mirror all you see is a spirit."

Gus continued to struggle with the idea of spirit; Conway could not figure out what he had said that Gus had interpreted "to blow away spirits you wave your hand," but the idea was a useful one.

Christmas Day was a great success. Gus loved his airport with planes and helicopters that really flew, a public address system that boomed out announcements, escalators that moved, searchlights that lit up and pivoted back and forth. Gina had a computer that answered thousands of questions and also functioned as an encyclopedia. One of the family treasures was the ring aunt Clare had received when she retired as president of Columbia University. Conway gave it to Samara. She had come of age.

12

The night of January second, Samara couldn't sleep. They were to fly back to Minneapolis the next morning and her obligations were again looming over her. It was good that they were going to have more space, but that might mean Yuri and Raisa would be more independent now, less helpful. Of course they wouldn't mean to be, but maybe they wouldn't see as clearly what needed to be done. And Ron might not really have forgiven her; things might not be the same.

However, the night of January third, back in St. Paul, she slept like a dead woman and woke up at seven perfectly refreshed. Surprisingly, the children slept well too and didn't awake until Samara had breakfast ready at seven-thirty. There were already two changes in the way things would work with Raisa and Yuri in their new apartment: Samara had slept in a room of her own and Raisa was not making breakfast. That second change might work out all right because Raisa got upset when the children wouldn't eat a big breakfast.

She must have been listening for sounds because as soon as Gina and Gus came piping into the kitchen, there was a knock on the door. "Come in," shouted the three as one.

"Oh you've got breakfast already. I could have done that."

"I can manage fine on Monday, Wednesday and Friday. But on Tuesday and Thursday I'll really be rushed. So why don't we divide the chore up. And maybe we can divide the weekend too so one day you can have the morning free and the other I can. After all, you have to do most of the other cooking."

Raisa smiled. "That would be nice. To have a break from cooking. Not that I mind. It's getting those rascals to eat that's more trouble."

"I know. It drove my mother wild."

That evening they set up Gus's airport in Marty's living room. Marty was delighted. Samara translated for the kids. "Marty says she wants one for her birthday."

Gus said, "Don't ask for an airport. You ask for a super runway and a super jet and a satellite launching pad. And then we can play together."

"Yes," Samara translated. "We don't need another airport."

Yuri said, "Raisa and I will put them to bed. You can stay down here and have a nice chat."

Samara told them about Gus's fear of Christmas.

"I suppose he's been subjected to the abnormal so the normal seems pretty good," Ron said.

Marty said, "He's probably a lot more alive to the spiritual world, the non-physical world, than most children."

"And the dangers there," Ron said.

"I think so. I can sense his relief at being back here. He just needs a home base, humdrum and stable, so much. I don't know what that means for the summer. Whether he could stand being moved to Summerland."

Marty said, "Ron and I have been talking about that. I couldn't afford to take such a long vacation again. Last summer really put the whole project behind. I'd talked myself into thinking I wasn't indispensable. But things go better when I'm around. Just because such a big project needs a leader."

"In one way, the summer was relaxing for you, but in another way it was tiring. Physically tiring," Ron said.

"Yes, I suppose so."

Samara said, "Something I've been meaning to ask and this is a good time. Are we tiring for you? I mean, we're not like an impersonal apartment tenant. There's the noise. And you're so much more involved."

"I don't know if it's tiring or not, but I love it. I love having a family, with children. We were a pretty sad lot while you were gone. The night before you were coming back Raisa and Yuri came down for supper, and we all were drunk with joy — we were so silly."

When Samara was ready to leave, Ron said, "I'll walk you upstairs." And at the door to the apartment, he said, "Can I come in for a minute or two?"

"Sure."

Raisa was sitting on the couch.

"How did they go to bed?"

"Like lambs. They seem so glad to be home. It quite thrilled me."

"They missed you, that's for sure."

"I'll be off now. But remember it's my turn to make breakfast. Just send them to knock on the door."

"Great," said Samara as Raisa left.

"I've got your present here." Ron took a small box from his pocket. In it was a necklace, seven twisted strands of brass with a pendant. On the pendant was engraved a cryptic symbol.

"Oh my. That's beautiful."

"I designed it myself."

"Does it mean something?"

"Yes, but you've got to figure it out."

The brass pendant was a triangle with rounded corners, three-dimensional, with a line that wrapped around the whole. There were arrow heads of a green stone at each end of the line. Samara contemplated it. It looked like a heart — a real one, at least like the only real heart Samara had ever seen, a chicken's. The line would then be a two-headed arrow, piercing the heart in two places.

On Sunday, there was a thumping on the floor and hollering. Raisa and Yuri burst in the door. "What is it?"

"It's downstairs. Hurry. Raisa, stay with the children."

Yuri and Samara tore down the stairs. Ron was kneeling over Marty, who had vomited and was now having great racking dry heaves. Her limbs were twitching wildly.

"Yuri, the ambulance. Samara, here. Stay." He ran off to Marty's room and came back with a syringe. He was drawing liquid from a little bottle into the needle. "Oh God. The swab. Samara, get the cotton. No, I'll get it. Hold this."

He came back with an antiseptic and swab. Yuri was back from the telephone. "Yuri, hold her arm out, still as you can." He scrubbed a patch of Marty's upper arm and took the needle from Samara. "Help him hold her arm still. I'm no good at this. Jesus Christ." He put the needle to her arm. "I can't do it. I've practiced so often on the damn doll and now I can't do it."

For her entire lifetime, Samara had practiced her mother's exercises. Now, from somewhere deep inside her, the result of these exercises began to assert itself. She stood up and began to hum, a strange low tune. She held Marty's hand loosely. Those nerves, she was thinking. Those poor battered nerves. Dear Lord, strengthen us. Strengthen our hearts. She continued to hum. Then she stopped. There was silence for fifteen or twenty seconds, a pause in Marty's heaving.

Samara was far away, in another country. Water was moving, a fountain, or a brook. Wind soughed through the spruce trees. Her mother was humming, the same low hum. There was another pause, of thirty seconds, in Marty's heaving. From this far-off land came Samara's voice, "Let not your heart be troubled, neither let it be afraid." Another silence. "Now Ron. Now you will be able to do it."

Ron, his chest tingling but his hands steady, plunged the needle into Marty's arm. When the needle was emptied, he took it into the bathroom and shut the door. Samara knelt at Marty's knee and spoke soothingly. "You're going to be fine. It's all right now." In another few minutes as Marty's twitching and heaving subsided, Samara said to Yuri, "Go into the other bathroom and get a towel. Or paper towels from the kitchen." Gently, Yuri cleaned Marty's lap. When he'd got up as much as he could, he put a clean towel over the stain.

While he was working, Samara gradually left the other land, but the air in the room seemed to have thickened with its calm.

Ron had developed diarrhea, so when the ambulance came, Samara went with Marty. She called in to Ron, "I've packed a nightgown and her medicine. When you're able, you come and bring what I've forgotten."

It was as Ron had feared. This vomiting was a signal that Marty's condition was worsening.

As Samara sat in the emergency ward waiting room, she thought about the calm she had been able to engender during the crisis. A healing efficacy, a soothing capacity, a concentrating power — these were mysterious qualities. What made a baseball hitter have a hot streak? Sometimes even an ordinary hitter rose to the occasion for an important series of games. What had happened to his whole person for those few days? Confidence, desire, a cause greater than himself.

And yet, Samara felt, somehow her presence had not helped Fred, not helped Marty in the long run, and even had hurt them, allowed some evil that had been kept at bay to invade them. Fred could give up because he realized she would take over the children. Marty might be, perhaps even unconsciously, worrying that Samara would steal Ron. Of course Marty loved him. That was obvious.

She couldn't move out. That would be destructive to Gina and Gus, even to Yuri and Raisa, who were all so happy there. And she didn't know if she could ignore Ron. That would make for a rift in the house. And be dishonest. Perhaps Marty would be reconciled if she and Ron became lovers but vowed never to leave her. But could all of them, the whole seven of them, live this way? Corruption would set in, discontent.

She would be guilty of pride if she believed that she herself had calmed the crisis and saved Marty. But I do have a kind of healing power, she thought. I just have to put my knowledge of the fact in the back of my head, not dwell on it; and only when I'm led to it, let myself become an instrument. Damn, I don't want to be that kind of person — goody goody, pure. I want to be an ordinary person, have fun the way others do.

But there was no way out. She couldn't abandon the six of them, nor could she stay there and hurt them. Nothing else she could do with her life was more important than to help all these people to survive, to be happy.

A few days after Marty came home from the hospital, Ron asked Samara to sit with her while he shopped for groceries. Raisa, Yuri, and the children went along with him for the exercise because a cold spell had kept everyone indoors. Marty was still weak and talking tired her. Samara took her hand, and they sat together in silence. Then Samara began to talk, and as if some barrier, some restraint had been taken away, she began to tell of her worries. Darkness was falling, but she didn't rise to put on lights. She confessed her desire for an ordinary life, or rather, she said, her fear that she might miss something in life, miss youthful fun. She stopped when the thought of marriage, love, came into her head.

Marty gasped out, "What we have here — a miracle. The rest know your gift."

Samara patted Marty's hand in answer. She bent her head toward the hand and kissed it.

Marty said, "Ron loves you."

Samara shook her head, not no, nor yes.

"He'll never leave me. We must live together. You, Ron, me."

"Yes."

It's all over, Samara thought. The struggle is over. All things have been resolved. The solution, the resolution, has been so simple. So amazingly simple.

That evening Ron called up the stairs to Samara. "Come on down when you're finished with whatever you're doing."

When the children fell asleep, Samara came down. Marty was already in bed, her door uncharacteristically closed. But even though the living room was empty, Ron led Samara into his room and shut the door. He pulled the chair out from the desk. "Here, sit here." He sat on the edge of the bed.

"Marty talked to you."

"Yes."

"So what do you think?"

"About what she said?"

"Yeah."

"I don't know. I wondered what you thought."

"You know what I think. The important thing is what you think."

"I don't really know what you think."

"Of course you do. It's as obvious as the nose on my face. The whole damn world knows." He twined his fingers and snapped his knuckles.

Samara closed her eyes and lowered her head. What was he proposing? Marriage? Living together? Her moving down here into his bedroom? They'd hardly even kissed. He must like her physically. Why hadn't he made more effort? It was plain that she would have to manage things.

"I don't know what you are proposing. That's what I mean by I don't know." She saw his face darken, grimace. With that expression, he looks like a wolf, she thought. He exhaled heavily.

But it isn't fair of me to make him say it all, she thought. I'll just have to dive in, and if I'm making a fool of myself, well, I'll have to live with that. She said, "Were you meaning that sometime in the future we'd get married? Like we'd be engaged? And we'd all live here, sort of like one family?"

He raised his hands in a shrug. "Sure. And we wouldn't have to wait too long into the future."

"The only thing is, won't Marty feel bad? I don't mean jealous. But just bad. Because she does love you. I mean more than just as a friend."

"She'd never admit it. Maybe she will feel bad. She says no."

"What if someday she's cured? They found a cure for her condition?"

"We'll cross that bridge when we come to it. I'm afraid it would take a miracle." The dark grimace reappeared.

They're asking too much of me again. People are always asking too much of me, Samara thought. But then I'm getting used to it. It's a big step. I haven't talked it over with the others. But here goes. Samara said, "There are a lot of things like that to work out. But I think we can do it. I'd like to try."

"At last it's settled." He stood up, took her hand and pulled her up. He put his hands on her shoulder, leaned forward and kissed her. She kissed back. They embraced, kissed again. It was only later that Samara thought, Our first real kiss was to seal our engagement. That's like Muslims or something.

13

The time came for parent-teacher interviews, and the question arose, who should attend? Samara had gone in the fall, since the children had been given into her care. Raisa would like to go, but a conference of the five adults determined that it would be good to have a man attend this time, so that the teacher would know there was a male presence for Gus. They expected that any difficulty would be over him.

But they were wrong. He, it seemed, was cheerful, well-behaved, learning at an acceptable rate. Gina, on the other hand, was a different story. Samara and Yuri sat in front of the desk of Mr. Anderson, a thin man with a crooked smile. He said to Yuri, "You are also the child's guardian?"

"No," Samara said. "I am the legal guardian. Yuri is . . . ." She stopped because she couldn't think of a word to describe him. She looked at Yuri, a question in her eyes.

He answered, "We are five adults in our house. My partner, Raisa, and I assist Miss Bellmont with the raising of the children. And there are two others who assist as well. You have no doubt heard of one of them, Dr. Martha Peters, the physicist at the University of Minnesota Institute for Research."

"Oh yes."

Yuri continued, "The children, Gina and her brother Gus in Miss Appleby's class, are in an unusual position as you can see."

"Yes. I can see that. And perhaps that explains — well, it doesn't explain — but I mean . . . ." He stopped.

"There is some difficulty?" Yuri prompted.

"She seems to me to be troubled. She has great difficulty concentrating. It's not that she misbehaves. But she seems — worried would be a good word perhaps. When they are to be working, she stares at me, and I say Gina, have you finished the lesson, and she says no, and I say do you need help and she looks frightened, worried. When I take her aside to give her extra help, she seems not to comprehend what I am saying. And yet, every once in a while, for a whole day sometimes, she is right on top of things. Two weeks ago, we had a module on storytelling. I had each of the children get up and tell a story. Gina was by far the best. She held the whole class enthralled, and when she finished they clapped spontaneously. So I know she has the capacity. Perhaps there is a learning disability. Perhaps we should arrange to have her tested. I've already had the school nurse test her eyes and ears. They're normal."

Yuri said, "She should be tested. We'll see to that immediately. You must tell us how to proceed."

"I can arrange that. We have an excellent program. Set up for us, I should add, by the University."

Samara said, "Perhaps we could figure out why she's right on sometimes. Perhaps there's something at home — sleeping or her diet or worry. And of course, as I mentioned in the fall, she has gone through a severe dislocation with the death of her father."

Gus was very interested in what his teacher had said, what they had seen. But Gina didn't want to hear anything about it.

On the weekend, Samara said, "I'm going to take Gina off by herself today. I was thinking last night about it. Maybe she needs to get away from Gus. I'll take her somewhere tranquil. And then we'll go somewhere quiet for lunch. What do you think? Is that a good idea?"

Raisa said, "I am very worried. Yuri and I think she should be taken to a doctor. To a specialist. Don't we, Yuri? We do not like to interfere, but that is our opinion if you do not mind my giving it."

"No, I need your advice. We're in this together. And I'm just so grateful for your help. I hadn't thought about a doctor. But it could be medical, couldn't it. I was thinking more how maybe she needed more peace and quiet. And solitude. I think she was used to a very lonely life."

"That is true. And perhaps all by herself, she will be able to give some hint about her trouble."

In the car, Gina asked, "Why isn't Gus coming?"

"I thought it would be nice for you and me to have some time together."

"Why isn't Raisa coming?"

"Someone had to look after Gus."

"When are we coming back?"

"After lunch probably. We can come back whenever we want."

"Where's our lunch?"

"We'll eat in a restaurant."

"Why isn't Gus coming?"

"To the restaurant?"

"Yes."

"So we — you and I — can have a nice visit. All by ourselves. Isn't that a good idea?"

Gina was silent. After a while she said, "Why isn't Yuri coming?"

"I suppose he wanted to say with Raisa."

"Why isn't Gus coming?"

"You and I never get to talk all by ourselves. Gus is always butting in. This way we can talk as much as we want. And I just thought it would be nice. I thought you would have a good time."

Samara thought, Funny little girl, she hasn't even asked where we're going. Their destination had posed a problem — where could they go and walk indoors? A mall would be too noisy and confusing. Finally Marty had suggested, "Go see the new gardens. People say they're lovely. And then you can tell us if Ron could maneuver me around them."

The Elliott Gardens had only been open two months. When they'd built the new stadium, a group of Minneapolis boosters had bought the Metrodome to turn it into indoor gardens. Yuhio Kojun designed them; he had died in an automobile accident just a few days before the official opening.

Crossing the street, Gina took her hand out of Samara's and grasped two of Samara's fingers in a tight grip. She looked worried. What was it she feared? Samara paid the fee and followed the directions toward the main attraction, the Japanese garden. She pushed open the door; warm humidity and the smell of spring rushed out at them. Gina had not relaxed her grip; in fact, she had tightened it — a deathhold, Samara thought.

But as they stepped into the garden, Samara heard from

Gina an involuntary "Ahhh." Stepping stones and paths of white pebbles led them around the garden, between bushes with flaming red flowers, across an arched bridge onto an island, past stone lanterns, some squat and jolly, others tall and dignified. Although they knew they were in a finite space, the paths were hidden from each other so cleverly that they had the illusion of traversing a vast expanse. Gina did not say much, but her face was as lit up as a cherub's. They walked slowly, and she looked at everything. Turning a corner, they came upon a waterfall. Through some sleight of hand, some optical illusion, the waterfall looked high. "Let's sit here and watch," Samara said, indicating a stone bench. Gina snuggled up close and put her head against Samara's shoulder.

"Where are we?" she said. "Is this fairyland?"

"It seems like it, doesn't it. But no, this is the Elliott Gardens. They just made it."

"Can we bring Gus here?"

"Sure, next Saturday if you want."

"And Raisa and Yuri? And Ron and Marty?"

"I wonder if Marty could get around. Maybe it would be too bumpy. What do you think?"

"We could try."

"Look, in the pool there."

Gina got up to look in the direction of Samara's pointing finger. "It's fishes. Orange fishes. And black fishes." The waterfall splashed into the pool. Around the edge, white flowers bloomed, and some flowers spilled over into the water.

They sauntered along. At one point, they could look into a clump of bamboo and see three or four royal blue birds. They also caught a glimpse of a little house, and later, they came upon the front of the building. They walked up onto the porch, past a stone basin into which water was running from a bamboo pipe, and through a gate into a tea garden, contained and small, exquisite, with a wooden Buddha sitting near the fence. Bright green moss covered the ground, except along the path where a highly perfumed blue flower bloomed.

A little way past the teahouse, there was an expanse of stark beauty — huge strangely-shaped boulders, giving the illusion of hills and valleys, and around a corner a lake of white pebbles.

When they'd come out the other side of the Japanese garden, Samara said, "There is more — a night garden and an herb garden." She looked down at the pamphlet, "And a hedge maze. Oh, quite a few more. Or we could eat lunch. There's a restaurant here. What would you like to do?"

"We'll eat. Next week we'll come back and show Gus."

"That's a good idea."

They each decided to have a fruit salad plate. While they were waiting for the food, Samara said, "So that's pretty nice, hey?"

"There could be fairies there."

"I wouldn't be surprised. You can tell your class about it in show and tell. We'll have to get something from the souvenir shop so you can show while you tell."

Gina's face clouded over. "I'm not going to tell *them*."

"No?"

"No!"

"Why not?"

"Because."

"Because why?"

"They're nasty."

"Mr. Anderson isn't, is he? You could tell him."

"He's nasty too."

"Oh." Samara thought she wouldn't probe for the moment. "What part did you like the best?"

"What part did you?"

"I liked the waterfall pretty well."

"Me too. I liked the tea garden."

"I did too. That really was like fairyland. Like a magic garden," Samara said.

"I liked the brook."

"That was pretty."

"With the stump you said looked like a fairy castle."

"That was special. And the green moss."

When they were eating their Princess Pudding, Gina said, "Samara?"

"Yes?"

"This was a good idea."

"A wonderful idea."

"You're smart."

"Maybe I am!"

At the gift store, Gina picked out a red Buddha for Gus, a paperweight Japanese garden in a snowstorm for Raisa, and a bamboo whistle for Yuri.

"This costs a lot, Samara. Can we get something for Ron and Marty?"

"Sure, this is a special treat for you. A special day."

"Why?"

"Because I love you, I guess."

Gina leaned her head against Samara's side and rubbed her head into it.

They got a green Buddha for Ron and a dish garden for Marty.

"Now you have to pick out something for yourself."

"For me?"

"Of course."

Gina decided on a stuffed toy, a monkey with an impish grin, holding a sword.

A few nights later when Samara was putting the children to bed, Gina said, "Tomorrow is show and tell."

"Is that right?"

"Yes."

Samara was thinking hard, trying to find the right words. Finally she said, "Do you like show and tell?"

"No."

"Why not?"

"I don't know."

"Have you ever got up to show?"

"No."

"Someday you might like to."

"What would I wear?"

"Do the kids wear something special when they show and tell?"

"Yes."

"Something you don't have?"

"They wear their long dress."

"To school?"

"Yes."

"Goodness. Would you like a long dress? You could have one you know."

In the darkness, Samara could hear Gina swallowing hard. Then she detected sniffling. Gus said, "Gina's crying." Samara leaned over and kissed her cheek, feeling the wetness. She grasped the child's shoulders and raised her up, hugging her. Tears welled up in her own eyes.

She did not know whether they were weeping for the sorrow that the children of God had to bear or sobbing with relief; grieving for the heartache Gina was not able to reveal or giving thanks because this need had been brought to light and was so easily satisfied. Yuri and Raisa, standing in the doorway, listening to the weeping, did not know either.

The next day in Marty's office, Ron said, "Where are we going to find this dress?"

"I'm not sure. But I promised her we'd go shopping after school. Do you two want to come along?"

"Of course," Ron said. "Would we want to miss this momentous event?"

Armed with information from Marty's secretary, the seven householders went to the Cherrytree Mall. Such a crowd made shopping a little unwieldy. Gina was all for taking the first long dress they found, but she was persuaded to look around a bit longer. In the end, they purchased a red plaid dress, decorated at the neck with lace and a green velvet bow.

They stopped at a take-out restaurant on the way home, and bearing dress and pizza, they entered their house in a momentary triumph.